Jimmy has already grown used to being alone in his mid-twenties. One failed attempt at romance after another has left him both weary and defiantly independent. That is, until Luke stumbles into his life, flashing his adorably crooked smile and wielding his boyish charm. Jimmy stands no chance against the boy of his dreams.

All seems picture perfect, but as the dust settles and the reality of day-to-day life takes over, Jimmy's happily ever after begins to suffocate. Differences arise and disagreements become the norm as Jimmy and Luke navigate the sometimes-troubling waters of early adulthood.

MORE PERFECT

Daniel Janaka

A NineStar Press Publication

Published by NineStar Press
P.O. Box 91792,
Albuquerque, New Mexico, 87199 USA.
www.ninestarpress.com

More Perfect

Copyright © 2018 by Daniel Janaka
Cover Art by Natasha Snow Copyright © 2018

This is a work of fiction. Names, characters, places, and incidents are either the product of the author's imagination or are used fictitiously. Any resemblance to actual persons living or dead, business establishments, events, or locales is entirely coincidental.

All rights reserved. No part of this publication may be reproduced in any material form, whether by printing, photocopying, scanning or otherwise without the written permission of the publisher. To request permission and all other inquiries, contact NineStar Press at the physical or web addresses above or at Contact@ninestarpress.com.

Printed in the USA
First Edition
August, 2018

Print ISBN: 978-1-949340-60-0

Also available in eBook, ISBN: 978-1-949340-59-4

Warning: This book contains sexually explicit content, which may only be suitable for mature readers.

Special thanks to Terry Wolverton whose thoughtful
guidance helped me find my story.

The history of the living world can be summarised as the elaboration of ever more perfect eyes within a cosmos in which there is always something more to be seen.

-Teilhard de Chardin, *The Phenomenon of Man*

Chapter One

"I NEVER DO this right. It's like every time is the first time for me."

Jimmy struggled to quiet his shaking hands as Luke took a drag from the bowl, resting his free hand on the steering wheel. Jimmy had fantasized about being close to him for weeks, but the confidence he'd so naturally possessed in his daydreams was nowhere to be found, all the charisma and charm replaced instead with a resounding fear that shot through him like an electric charge of restlessness. His leg fidgeted, bobbing up and down to its own chaotic rhythm. His whole body trembled.

"It's freezing in here," he noted, hoping to hide his nerves behind the chill.

"Sorry, it takes a while for the heat to warm up." Luke reached for the air vent and adjusted its direction, guiding it toward Jimmy. "That should help."

Luke pulled another waft of smoke deep into his lungs, holding it in for a few seconds before gently releasing it into the air. Jimmy watched out of the corner of his eye, trying not to stare but unable to look away. Luke's adorably lanky arms remained suspended for a moment as he emptied his lungs. His skin was pale, his nostrils highlighted by a soft pink glow. His shaggy hair crowned his boyish frame, an unorchestrated mound of waves and curls.

The streetlight above flickered, struggling to illuminate the quaint Brooklyn neighborhood, abnormally free of any distraction. No pedestrians, no traffic, none of the usual late-night clamor. The hybrid cinema-bar was only a block ahead. Its sign shone in the distance as Jimmy peered through the dirty windshield.

A group of rowdy men exited, interrupting the silence with their laughter as one man pulled out a cigarette before passing the pack along. The twenty-minute intermission between screenings provided a welcome opportunity to grab a smoke, use the bathroom, or be alone with a dangerously captivating new friend.

It had been a challenge to quiet his overactive mind while trapped in the dark theater—sitting so close, feeling the accidental graze of Luke's arm against his own. He had been forced to keep his eyes fixed on the screen ahead as he struggled to absorb the subtitles that fired off one after another while his mind ran in circles, left only to imagine those puffy eyes surrounded by soft dark circles like remnants of a constant lack of sleep. When the first film had reached its finale—the score rising in an unnecessarily epic crescendo—the lights slowly rose, illuminating the sparsely filled space.

Jimmy hid a yawn as Luke leaned in and whispered, "I don't want to sound like a freak, so of course no pressure, but I have some pot in my car if you want to smoke a little before the next one. It might be more fun to watch it with a buzz."

It didn't exactly fit the construct of what Jimmy had in mind for the evening, but the warmth of Luke's breath as it grazed against his ear thwarted any desire to refuse. It had, however, been some time since his last encounter with the unpredictable herb. He grew concerned about what he might do or say while stoned, fearful that the smallest dent in his armor of coolness could send Luke running back to Jersey.

Jimmy took the pipe, silently commanding his hands to cease their incessant shaking. His fingers grazed Luke's in the exchange.

"Just pull it in, and let it sit in your lungs for a while before you let it out." Luke reached over and took Jimmy's hand, guiding it around the pipe in the right direction. His fingers were long and slender but knotted at the knuckles; his fingernails short and frayed, jagged around the edges. He placed Jimmy's thumb over the small hole at the side of the pipe. "You've got to cover the hole when you pull in at first," he explained.

Jimmy willingly took instruction, delighted to be touched. He pulled in a small, apprehensive drag and waited for a moment, holding the smoke in his lungs as he had been instructed to do. He glanced over at Luke who to his surprise was smiling in approval. Jimmy smiled back as he admired Luke's childlike expression, more a grin than a smile whereby only the left side of his mouth was raised. There was something sinister about it, devious even, but charming. Steadily, Jimmy exhaled.

"There you go," Luke exclaimed. "You got it."

Jimmy smiled and flicked the lighter again, already a pro. He pulled in another drag, this one bigger.

"Now we're talking," cheered Luke.

A ball of fire barreled down Jimmy's throat, scorching the terrain as it made its way to his lungs and filled them beyond capacity. He hurried to exhale but began coughing, his insides erupting as heavy clouds of smoke burst out. He heaved for air between attacks, desperately trying to regain composure.

"It's—I took—oh, man." His eyes filled to the brim.

Luke chuckled and placed a caring hand on Jimmy's shoulder, holding back his amusement while he offered support.

The coughs grew fainter and the outburst subsided. Jimmy's breathing returned to normal. He dried his eyes and sat upright, eager to recover. His head was lighter. Time began to crawl. He passed the bowl back to Luke who received it with another half smile before the glass vessel met his mouth. Luke cradled it with only the tips of his long, delicate fingers. His rosy lips puckered as he released another effortless stream of smoke. He moved with such precision, his methodical gestures casting a spell on Jimmy as he imagined Luke's moist lips pressed against his own, pot-flavored saliva mixing.

Luke turned to Jimmy, catching him midstare.

Jimmy looked away, gearing his attention ahead.

Silence lay awkwardly suspended between the two. Jimmy's leg sprang into action, bobbing up and down chaotically as he struggled to come up with something to say, anything to distract from his embarrassment. It was his dead dog, Sneakers, who entered his mind at that particular moment, becoming the topic of his incomprehensible rant. He anxiously traversed the subject, hoping that as long as he continued he might find a point, some meaningful way of making the story relevant.

Luke charged forward.

He pounced without warning, catching Jimmy off guard, a dangling word about Sneakers still struggling to escape, quashed by Luke's eager lips. Jimmy sat frozen, suspended in a state of shock as his lips acquiesced. His eyes remained wide open. He glanced around to assess the situation in hopes of regaining consciousness. Luke's eyes were sealed shut. Jimmy closed his.

Luke grabbed Jimmy's face, pulling him closer. Jimmy kissed harder, adding his tongue to the mix in hopes of returning to his body and ending the sudden, ill-timed fit of numbness. Luke accepted, offering his tongue as well. It twirled around Jimmy's, slithering in and out of his mouth with skill. The haze was lifting. Jimmy reached over, trying to touch Luke's face, but Luke's arms created an impenetrable barrier. He settled for his elbows before eventually resting his hands on Luke's thigh. Jimmy caressed Luke's leg as a rush of excitement filled him. Blood charged through his body. His senses now on overdrive, he could finally taste the boy attached to him, feel his moistness. He lunged forward, pushing Luke back into his seat. His hands were now free to roam as they pleased. He ran them up and down Luke's torso, traversing his stomach and chest until resting on Luke's face. Luke moaned softly. Jimmy leaned in farther, pressing closer, wincing in pain as the center console stabbed into his side, but continued on his mission to devour him.

Luke pushed forward, sending Jimmy crashing into the steering wheel.

The horn burst into action.

Their mouths broke apart as they surrendered to laughter, the tips of their noses still touching. Jimmy peered behind and noticed the men near the theater staring. He peeled away.

"I guess we should get going?" Jimmy suggested.

"I guess," Luke replied as he wiped the sides of his mouth clean. "Don't want to miss the next one."

Jimmy's heart pounded as he exited the car, flattening his shirt and rearranging his hair.

Luke approached, offering his hand.

Jimmy placed his hand in Luke's, quieting his enthusiasm as best he could as they began down the sidewalk. Their fingers locked together as a sense of ease washed over him. There was no concern for the group of men watching as they approached. He no longer worried about being awkward or unprepared. The chatter of his overactive mind had quieted.

They entered the theater, still joined together, and took seats in the back row.

"More privacy back here," Luke said with a wink.

Jimmy smiled brightly, unable to contain his excitement as the lights dimmed.

A LOUD AND sustained beep snapped Jimmy back to reality.

He stared down at the massive copier. A few pages struggled to escape from the machine's slim slot, the words PAPER JAM blinking ominously on the small screen. He tugged fiercely at the wad of copies until finally freeing them from their captor, and then gathered the pages and made his way out of the copy room. It had been some time since he had remembered Luke, a boy so removed from his present day he now seemed like a figure of his imagination. But somehow, Luke returned, offering Jimmy's idle mind a moment of stimulation.

He walked past the bullpen of designers, most packing their things and scurrying out of the office, clearly ready to start the weekend, and arrived at the reception desk where he arranged the copies, discarding the wrinkled ones and placing the others squarely atop a pile of prints. The hardwood floors, scuffed and scraped from years of abuse, moaned as the office cleared. The sounds of movement bounced against the concrete walls and exposed ceiling like noises in a cave. The cries of the upheaval were muted only by the Kilim area rugs laid throughout the loftlike space, the vibrant colors and bold tribal prints only adding to the eclectic mix of sights and sounds. Jimmy smiled for a moment, taking it all in—the Friday evening rush.

Making copies and answering phones was never part of his master plan. He had imagined that by twenty-four he would be an adult with a significant job and a life to go with it. Instead, he spent most of his days directing phone calls and organizing lunch orders. When he had first interviewed at Freestyle Initiative, a boutique graphic design house, as hip as the décor of the office, he had been certain he'd found his place. It would only be a matter of time until they realized his potential, he thought. Only a matter of time until he was one of the designers, being creative and doing what he loved.

Instead, he remained stuck at the front desk, left only to examine the work others were creating, taking mental note of things he liked and things he would have done differently. He thought about leaving from time to time but dreaded the idea of starting over. He was, for the most part, happy enough. And there was Michael, his boss, who still managed to lull Jimmy into a state of complacency.

Jimmy had taken notice of the rugged, yet refined founder of Freestyle from the moment they'd shaken hands at his initial interview almost two years ago. By the time the meeting was over and Michael said in his deep, caring voice, "You'll start on Monday," Jimmy had been bewitched.

It'd been by no means the first time he had too quickly imagined feelings for a stranger. A simple glance from any worthwhile passerby was more than enough to send his imagination soaring. It had once been the friendly clerk at his local grocery store whose pearly-white smile seemed to be a definite sign of interest. On another occasion, it had been the new tenant in his building, who greeted Jimmy with a lingering handshake, too prolonged to go unnoticed.

"You're still here?" Michael asked as he made his way to the elevator, leaving now that the office was nearly vacant, the chaotic bustling slipping into silence.

Jimmy had found it hard, at first, to manage his infatuation for Michael. His breath shortened whenever they were alone, his leg twitched uncontrollably. But his desires had subsided as they developed a familiarity with one another, becoming colleagues and even friends. Jimmy most appreciated their moments alone, the two lost in their own world as they discussed in private the men passing in and out of Michael's life, whispering so as not to be heard by the rest of the office.

"I'll be leaving soon," Jimmy replied with a smile.

Michael was wearing a new shirt. He had likely changed behind closed doors, perhaps preparing for a date. It fit snug around his toned frame, buttoned all the way to the top. His pronounced Adam's apple grazed against his collar as it rose and fell. Michael wished Jimmy well with a smile as the elevator doors closed, whisking away the dapper man along with the sounds of haste. The office was finally quiet.

Jimmy leaned back in his chair, taking in the moment of peace, a rare find in a city as bustling as New York. He would soon have to make his way to the subway station at Union Square, fending against the calamity of rush hour, squeezing too close to strangers as he journeyed to Charlie's apartment in Brooklyn. He dreaded the forced conversations with Charlie's friends, people he barely knew, the copious amounts of alcohol he would undoubtedly have to ingest in order to stay engaged. How easy it would be to take the train to Queens instead, to make his way home and cuddle up in front of the TV. But he had promised his friend, and he was already late.

Chapter Two

ARRIVING AT A party alone was most often a discomfort worth avoiding. Jimmy creeped through the empty hallway. Muffled chatter and the tedious pounding of bass filled the ever-narrowing space, getting louder as he inched toward the apartment door.

He felt the piercing glare of critical eyes burning through his flesh as soon as he entered. A group of strangers lined the wall near the front door, staring him up and down. He walked past the kitchen, trying to moderate his haste. He moved to the small living room, hopeful that Charlie was somewhere near. The apartment was emptier than the filtered noise from the hallway let on, the crowd too sparse to get lost in. Jimmy's every move was being observed. He was sure of it, and Charlie was nowhere in sight. He stood aimless in the middle of the living room. The couch, the most obvious place for retreat, was fully occupied, and there was little space to linger anywhere else. He turned toward the window at the other end of the apartment, contemplating an escape. Surely, there was a fire escape he could scale down.

A smack landed squarely on his ass. "Finally! Where have you been?" Charlie snarled.

Jimmy hugged Charlie, enlivened with relief as he blamed Michael for being late.

"I thought you were flaking out on me."

"I would never," Jimmy replied. "Where's Blake?"

"Not coming. Can you believe it?"

"What is with these pants?" Jimmy asked, peering down at Charlie's outfit.

Charlie twirled around, showing off his new jeans. "Denim in the front. Leather in the back! Isn't it awesome?"

Jimmy had always admired Charlie's confidence. He was sure of himself in a way that Jimmy could only hope to be. The jeans fit snug around his tiny waist, accentuating his perky ass.

"You're rocking the shit out of them like only you can."

"Aw—thanks, babe. Come on. Let's get you a drink."

Charlie took Jimmy's hand and ushered him to the kitchen where a group of young boys, smooth and glistening, were clearing out, plastic cups freshly filled. As the space cleared, a tall, striking man lingered. From the looks of it, he was older than the rest of the crowd, possibly in his thirties. He braced against the refrigerator as Charlie and Jimmy entered.

Charlie pushed the lonely laggard out of the way. "Move, Robert. I need to get in my fridge."

"Okay, okay," Robert responded with a chuckle. He extended his hand toward Jimmy, introducing himself.

Robert's dark-brown skin, a unique blend of ethnicities, was flawless. Clear and smooth, without a single blemish. It begged to be touched. His jet-black hair was tailored to perfection, tightly framing his strong, angular face. His eyes were such a faint shade of gray they almost appeared to be clear, the irises nearly blending in with the white that surrounded them. His gaze was mesmerizing, haunting even.

Jimmy greeted him with restrained enthusiasm, dropping his voice an octave lower in an effort to match Robert's warm and soothing tone. "I'm James," he offered.

The use of *James* was normally reserved for professional settings, but there was something about Robert's demeanor that demanded authority, rendering *Jimmy* inadequate.

Charlie geared his attention to Jimmy, giving a knowing glare as he handed him a plastic cup filled nearly to the brim with beer.

"Jimmy's my partner in crime," Charlie told Robert before continuing to lay out a list of worthy attributes, offering Jimmy to the potential buyer like an item on an auction block.

Jimmy squirmed under the spotlight's glow, relieved only when Charlie reached the end of his presentation and sauntered out of the kitchen, leaving him alone with the handsome stranger.

"It's all smoke and mirrors," he joked, shifting from side to side.

"Sounds like you guys are pretty close," Robert replied. "Why haven't I seen you around before?"

"I don't really like people. Don't find them worth the effort."

Robert laughed. The stark whiteness of his perfectly aligned teeth was almost blinding. "I'm glad you decided to make an exception tonight."

"I'm just here for the free beer," Jimmy said, raising his cup in the air before taking a large gulp.

Robert's attention remained fixed as he interrogated Jimmy, asking what he did and where he lived. He leaned close, his entrancing eyes singularly focused. A certain comfort sprang up between them. Robert, unlike Charlie's other friends, was easy to talk to. Despite being intimidatingly good-looking, he possessed a certain nonchalance that put Jimmy at ease. The two chatted privately, hidden away in the kitchen as minutes passed effortlessly. Jimmy relished listening to Robert's soothing baritone as he imagined their naked bodies pasted together in the heat of passionate lovemaking.

The handsome stranger was mature, more experienced in life than most at the house party. Jimmy asked his age.

Robert smiled. "Take a guess."

"Twenty-six?" he replied, though he was certain Robert was older.

"Twenty-eight."

"I was close! I'm actually relieved to know you're not eighteen. Seems like the crowd here is a little younger than the two of us."

"Charlie has a wide range of friends," Robert replied, his piercing gaze studying hard. "I thought you were younger. You've got a very young look about you." His words slithered with intent toward Jimmy's ears.

"So I've been told." Jimmy's palms moistened as he meekly took another gulp from the plastic cup. "I tried growing out a beard, but it didn't really take."

Robert smiled again, his face glowing. "You should be happy you look young. People always assume I'm in my thirties."

"I think I'd rather that." Jimmy was now certain Robert's flirtation was more than just imagined. "Being older affords you more respect."

"In some settings."

"Yeah, maybe not here." Jimmy leaned in closer, eager to close the distance between their bodies. "We're ancient," he whispered.

Robert laughed softly, leaning in farther, allowing his nose to nearly graze Jimmy's cheek. His breath blanketed Jimmy's skin in warmth, causing his body to tingle with anticipation as he inhaled the strong scent of the man's cologne. He waited for their lips to crash together, imagining his hands gliding against Robert's smooth, supple skin. His heart raced at the thought of their bodies colliding as a palpable silence grew. Robert's breath filled the space between them, the intensity of it mounting. Jimmy licked his lips, preparing for the inevitable union.

Robert pulled away. "Well, here's to being ancient." He raised his cup in the air. "At least we're not in it alone," he added. His playful, sexual tone abruptly retreated—triggered, it seemed, by some internal alarm. Jimmy remained silent for a moment, confused about the sudden change in climate, worried he had unknowingly missed his chance. Perhaps, he thought, he should be more forward, make a move. Maybe Robert was waiting for a sign he had not yet received.

"I should get going," Robert said. "My boyfriend is at home sick and I promised him soup."

Jimmy's attention sharpened and his eyes widened. The word *boyfriend* rang in his ear. His stance fell in defeat as he waited for an explanation. Robert offered none. His head now lowered like a guilty puppy, Robert stared into his nearly empty plastic cup. Jimmy's confusion turned to frustration. He had been fooled, duped into believing something was brewing. It was a disappointing realization he knew all too well, but he refused to appease the situation by brushing it off with feigned indifference. Instead, they stood in silence for a tense, lingering moment.

"It was really nice meeting you, James," Robert finally uttered.

Jimmy forced a smile. "You too," he murmured, finishing the rest of his beer with one swift gulp.

Robert moved closer and hesitated for a moment before wrapping his arms around Jimmy. His grasp was firm. He pressed his body tightly, his hand supporting Jimmy's back as they remained connected. Despite being agitated by the misdirection, Jimmy could not deny the joy of feeling the man against him. He allowed his face to graze Robert's. His skin was as soft as he'd suspected.

Robert's lips moved close to Jimmy's ear as he whispered, "Stay in touch, okay?"

Jimmy nodded, unable to form words.

Before separating, Robert pressed his moist lips against Jimmy's cheek, kissing him delicately. "I really hope to see you around, James."

Robert drifted away, the tall, dark stranger swallowed by the crowd in the hallway, the heat of lost possibilities still pressed against Jimmy's skin.

"Did he leave?" Charlie asked as he popped back into the kitchen.

Jimmy stared blankly at his friend for a moment, the moistness from Robert's lips on his cheek. "Yeah."

"Strange," Charlie replied. "He is fucking gorgeous, isn't he?"

Jimmy shook off the fantasy with a grin.

"Where'd he go?" Charlie asked.

"Home. To see his boyfriend."

"That's right," Charlie responded, suddenly remembering the crucial bit of information. "Well, what happened? Did you jerk him off right here in my kitchen?"

Jimmy wiped his cheek clean.

"He totally wants to lick your ass," Charlie added.

"He's got a boyfriend!" Jimmy barked.

"I didn't say marry the guy."

JIMMY'S NEIGHBORHOOD WAS quiet when he got back to Queens. It was always more still there. He emerged from the station and opted for the long way home through the park to take in the night. He crossed a large intersection lined with trees and wandered through an open space of grass. The park was empty, as always at night, covered in darkness, but peaceful. Even behind shadows, the deep green of the landscape was inviting, unlike Charlie's neighborhood in Brooklyn, made-up almost entirely of concrete and stone. He lingered for a while before continuing. Along the way, he passed rows of old houses. Some were updated, some left in their original state, houses filled with families who had likely occupied the space for decades, handing it down from one generation to the next. There was comfort in the quaintness of suburbia amidst the roaring calamity of the city. It reminded him, in some ways, of the Long Island street he'd grown up on, where his parents still lived. Despite having been enamored with the city when he first left home, he'd somehow found his way to a place that felt like the past.

His apartment was in perfect order when he returned, everything in its place as it always was—a safe haven of his own making. Jimmy appreciated the tranquility living alone provided. He liked silence, for the most part. But at times, when loneliness settled in, it could be deafening. There were times he wished he might arrive home to find someone waiting for him, times when he longed for more than just stillness. But, despite his best efforts, his loneliness appeared to have no end. Try as he might, he seemed doomed to endure one false start after another, each time foolishly hopeful that the answer to his sadness was within reach. Luke remained the harshest of those blows. With Luke, Jimmy had been close to finding it, or so he'd thought at the time.

Mutual friends had set them up, and to Jimmy's surprise, it'd been a well-conceived match. Their eyes connected as soon as Luke entered the small café, wearing an oversized button-down, the end of the shirt almost falling to his knees. The tips of his Converse sneakers barely peeked out from under the heavy legs of his baggy jeans. He looked like a little boy buried in men's clothing. He was lanky, his build not unlike Jimmy's. His arms dangled at his side as he walked, the sleeves of his puffy dress shirt rolled up to his elbows.

The adorably awkward Luke grinned as he approached Jimmy and introduced himself. His features were delicate except for his thick, full eyebrows, the intensity of their blackness a stark contrast to the otherwise cool tone of his face. His lips were dainty, feminine even—such a brilliant shade of pink they seemed to glow against his pale, porcelain skin, not a blemish or sign of stubble in sight. His nose was long, pointed at its tip. A faint darkness surrounded his puffy brown eyes. Jimmy's body tingled with warmth as Luke settled in and fidgeted with his place setting.

Usually, anxiety took over when with someone as absorbing as Luke, the incessant working of his neurosis sending him down a rabbit hole of self-doubt as he calculated, forming lists in his head of all the ways he was inadequate. But with Luke, it was different. There was no suffocating need to say the right thing, no reason to monitor his mannerisms or tailor his personality to whatever ideal he deemed appropriate. He was instantly himself, at ease.

When they were through with lunch, they stood outside, nearly ready to part ways. The constant flow of conversation came to a natural end and was replaced with a comfortable silence—one both seemed reluctant to leave behind. Luke stood on the curb, hovering over Jimmy. He stared intently without words, his eyes saying more than he was willing to divulge. Jimmy considered looking away, averting his attention from a face that shone so brightly in his direction, but couldn't. He was happy to stare back. Luke's hands were pressed into his pockets, arms straight, as he swayed back and forth, getting close and then pulling away. Jimmy's heart pounded.

Then the swaying stopped and Luke leaned in to whisper, "Let's do this again. Sometime soon hopefully."

Things moved quickly after the first meeting. Luke sent a text the next day—a small, cordial greeting to test the waters that led to longer conversations, some spanning days. Jimmy grew giddy whenever his phone buzzed, distracting him at work and home, his every thought focused on Luke. Though it was immediately palpable, this something between them, he tried hard not to get carried away, aware that it was far too early to safely indulge. The battle within continued for days as conflicting emotions piled on top of each other, creating a tower of confusion that he struggled to endure. A sense of doom hovered above, tainting every action and thought with uncertainty. He read every text message over and over again, carefully devising and revising his replies. It was suffocating, this level of worry, but he sensed the weight of possibility heavy on his shoulders. Its fragility required a certain level of care. He had to be cautious not to screw it up.

They wasted no time, meeting again the following weekend, kissing for the first time in Luke's car, lying together shortly after. Jimmy was cautious about sex. The few times before had been with near strangers, encounters that hardly mattered. Luke was different, and he avoided rushing into anything, certain that they would explore all aspects of intimacy as time progressed. But time, as it turned out, was not on his side.

There was no gradual decline, no prelude to the end. It came, instead, to a screeching halt, knocking Jimmy over like a ton of bricks. They were sitting on the couch in Jimmy's old apartment. His laptop and a carefully prepared tray of cheese and crackers rested on a makeshift coffee table only inches away. The movie they had been watching finished, and Luke sprang up from the chair.

Jimmy had felt the coldness growing all day, the air between them tense. Luke had been distant. Something inside him seemed to recoil, his once relaxed ease replaced with an anxious restlessness, his interest waning. Luke scrambled to grab his sneakers, thrusting his feet into them as he spoke. Jimmy stood up, joining him at the door.

"I'm visiting my sister out of town next weekend," Luke said. "But let's hang out when I'm back."

Jimmy struggled to smile, desperate to overcome the confusion building up behind the mask. He knew the invitation was an empty one. There would be no next time. It was slipping away from him, but he could do nothing to return things to the way they were.

"Do you want me to walk you down?" he asked. "I can wait for the subway with you."

"No, don't worry. I think I'm going to take a cab to the Path. It's late."

Jimmy stood at his doorway as Luke walked down the long, dimly lit corridor. As he turned the corner about to make his way down the stairs, Luke turned back for a moment and waved his final goodbye.

Jimmy shut the door behind him and returned to his empty apartment, the untouched tray of crackers and cheese on his coffee table seeming to laugh at him, a cruel reminder of his failure. The air rushed out of his chest as he sank to the floor. His back rested against the cold apartment door.

He shut his eyes, squeezing them tight and cursing the universe for dangling a dream so close only to rip it away.

Jimmy remained unraveled for some time thereafter, confused and wounded, spending countless hours retracing his steps in hopes that he might discover a cause, some understandable reason for Luke's disappearance. When he finally gave up his search for answers, he took to dating, making every effort to meet new people in hopes that Luke might just be one of many. He was certain he could find it again. If his short-lived, ill-fated fling had proven anything, it was that it existed—that thing he was searching for. It was out there in the world, waiting to be found. But, as he had feared, none measured up. There were men he admired, ones he detested, others he lusted after, but none who felt like home.

Chapter Three

"ALL SET FOR the meeting?" Jimmy asked as his boss emerged from the elevator.

Michael was dressed more formally than usual. His tailored shirt was tucked into his freshly pressed slacks. His shoes gleamed as though having just been shined.

"I think so," Michael said as he pulled his laptop from his bag and rested it in front of Jimmy. "But I need another set of eyes on this." He leaned in, hovering over the screen, only inches from Jimmy. The scent of his earthy cologne was sharp but sweet. Jimmy swallowed hard as he struggled to focus on the images before him, design ideas for the opening title sequence of a new reality show, which documented a group of young makeup artists living and working in New York. Michael had been thrilled when he'd secured the meeting with the producers. Even Jimmy was excited. It was the first project of its kind, and getting the job would mean a significant spike in the company's notoriety.

"I like it," Jimmy said with a hint of poorly masked doubt.

"Please. Tell me how you really feel," Michael insisted.

Jimmy gave it some thought before replying, mentally constructing the best expression of his reservations. It lacked any sort of unique perspective. It felt like the opening to any other reality show, except instead of houses or food, the images were of models and makeup. Jimmy hoped it would be fresher, hipper, something more in line with what the company was known for. Michael had overthought it, his nerves likely getting the best of his otherwise impeccable taste, and ended up imitating the norm as opposed to being true to his own voice.

Jimmy offered his thoughts, careful not to overstep. Michael was receptive as he absorbed Jimmy's perspective. But his frustration was growing.

"Shit. That's what I was worried about," he said as he slammed his laptop shut. "It's completely uninteresting. I've got to come up with something else before this evening."

Jimmy shifted in his chair, trying to find some words of comfort, but came up short.

"I'll send you the project," Michael continued. "Why don't you play around with some ideas, too, and we'll see what adjustments we can make before lunch."

Jimmy widened his eyes as he sprang to attention. He nodded, still in shock as Michael scurried into his office. Jimmy bolted toward his computer once alone and stared at the glowing screen. Michael had, in the past, asked for his opinion, but he had never before enlisted Jimmy to help design anything. Jimmy swallowed hard as he revved himself up to work, worrying all the while that his ideas were trite, amateurish, reaching for something beyond his grasp. It was crucial he put his best foot forward. He could, after all, lose Michael's trust if he came up with something laughable, making it a first and last chance to be noticed. But there was no time to doubt. He worked diligently, his leg bouncing beneath his desk like a metronome keeping rhythm until it was time to show Michael what he had come up with.

Michael smiled, seemingly surprised by the outcome of Jimmy's hard work. "These are great," he affirmed, squeezing Jimmy's shoulder. "I'm almost done with my revisions. I think we've got what we need to make this work."

The meeting started two hours late. The Los Angeles–based clients had travel delays and arrived behind schedule. They were short and abrupt, cutting Michael off midsentence at times. Jimmy stood by in disbelief as his boss tried to grab their attention. Michael's quaff of golden hair fell in front of his face as he leaned down again and again to attend to his laptop.

One of the clients, an overweight man in his midfifties, balding with sparse gray hairs protruding from the side of his head, seemed particularly frustrated. "It just seems confusing to me. There's so much going on, I don't know where to look. It's hard to imagine what it will ultimately look like when it's finished, but this doesn't seem like what we talked about." The others in the room nodded in support, the man's opinion clearly carrying weight.

Michael geared his attention to the image on the large screen behind him and stared at it for a moment as if now seeing it in a new light. His stance deflated ever so slightly. When he turned back to the group, his attention landed squarely on Jimmy.

"I understand," Michael replied. "I do have two other ideas that we've been toying with."

Jimmy's heart jumped into his throat as his work popped up on the enormous screen. The conference room grew quiet.

"Now this is cool," the balding man proclaimed. He leaned close to the woman near him, conferring with her privately.

Michael shot Jimmy a glance, his eyebrows raised, an anxious grin plastered on his face. When the man returned his attention to the front of the room, Michael clicked to the next slide, Jimmy's second design, and explained his idea for the new concept.

The man nodded. "It's not perfect, but this is the direction we need to be heading in. Let's flesh this out and see where we land."

Michael agreed, holding back an emerging smile. Jimmy's breath froze. When the clients finally cleared the room, Michael approached and gave Jimmy an ecstatic high five.

"You killed it!" he exclaimed.

Jimmy smiled brightly. "I can't believe they liked it!"

"You saved my ass. Thank you, James. It's going to be you and me on this one."

Michael exited the room. The echo of his praise rang in Jimmy's ears. His work still shone on the screen. It had been seen and appreciated, most importantly by Michael. He stood tall in the conference room, more sure of himself than ever before. The usual, resounding clamor of self-doubt quieted as a sense of purpose arose, filling him with inspiration.

Chapter Four

JIMMY'S UMBRELLA STOOD no chance against the heavy winds. It turned inside out, the frail metal bars snapping in two almost as soon as he stepped outside. He pulled at one end as Mother Nature grabbed the other, fighting to claim it as her own. Finally, when he was adequately drenched from head to toe, he gave up the struggle and surrendered the useless umbrella to the nearby trash can.

Charlie laughed as Jimmy entered the restaurant, water dripping from the ends of his lifeless hair. Jimmy was in no mood to make light of the situation.

"Let's just eat," he said as he rolled his eyes. "I have to be back at work in an hour."

"I'm just happy you could meet me in the middle of the day. This is rare for you."

He had grown accustomed to longer lunch breaks since his pseudo-promotion at Freestyle. They hadn't managed to land the Los Angeles account, but Michael was impressed enough with Jimmy's work to hire an intern to help alleviate much of the workload at the front desk, giving Jimmy time to collaborate with the creative department throughout the day, sitting in on meetings, peering over the designers' workstations when they would allow it.

"I'm happy we're finally meeting up," Jimmy said as he admired Charlie's beaming glow. "I feel like I haven't seen you in forever."

Charlie was a changed man since securing a boyfriend, calmer and noticeably more optimistic. Jimmy admired how willingly his friend had taken to settling down. It was not Charlie's usual way to couple up and domesticate, but in this new relationship, he'd seemed to discover happiness. Jimmy found it inspiring, even if it did mean losing his partner in crime. His weeks, usually filled with happy hour cocktails and Sunday morning brunches, were replaced with lonely movies and introspective walks around the city. He did his best not to get agitated when Charlie ignored his calls or waited days to reply to a text. His friend's priorities had changed. It was only natural, Jimmy assured himself. Still, feeling tossed aside was hurtful. At times, he longed to talk to Charlie, to really express how he felt, but whenever they did get together, it was like no time had passed. The months spent growing apart vanished, and they fell into old habits, laughing like they had when they still saw each other every week.

"So can you come out with us tonight?" Charlie asked as he inhaled the last bite of his tuna melt.

"I've got class tonight," Jimmy replied, "but maybe this weekend."

"You're still taking that class?"

"I've only got a couple more sessions. Figure I should at least try to get my money's worth."

THE RAIN HAD stopped by the time the workday was through. His jacket was mostly dry. Only his socks remained wet, squishing and squashing in his shoes as he made his way to class. When he arrived, the small group of fellow students were already hard at work, eyes glued to bright computer monitors, peering forward every once in a while to check their work against the example at the front of the room. Jimmy sat in the back and pried his feet from his shoes, letting his soggy socks air dry underneath the desk.

His attention was far less fixed as he worked. The assignment was easy, too easy. He had hoped, when he first signed up for the class, learning more about video production might grant him a leg up at work as television content began to dominate the company's workload. Some sort of formal training would be helpful, he'd thought, but lessons were progressing at a painfully slow rate. He was certain he could do better on his own, learning from videos on YouTube. But he had already paid for the classes, so he continued to attend, week after week.

After reaching the assignment's end and getting the required approval from the somewhat absentminded instructor, he gathered his things and exited the quiet room, eager to find something to eat and call it a night. The desolate hallway was drab and gloomy as always. Pale shades of brown lined the walls like dirt coverings. The gray industrial carpeting was torn and stained. An air of abandonment filled the space. Perhaps it was once home to a thriving business, maybe in the seventies when brown walls would have been acceptable. Now it seemed void of any life. He darted through the long corridor, not wanting to spend any more time in its eeriness than was necessary, when a voice called out to him, shouting his name from a distance. It echoed through the cavernous hallway, bouncing off the narrow walls.

The corridor seemed to elongate to an unseen vanishing point when Jimmy turned around. In the distance was a figure scurrying toward him. Its long arms flailed in the air as it gained traction.

"Luke?" Jimmy whispered, questioning if his mind was playing tricks on him. He had mistakenly spotted Luke time and time again, always to a disappointing end. Jimmy took a breath, hoping to return his heart to its rightful place in his chest. The hallway contracted, returning to normalcy as Luke's stride slowed upon arrival.

"Jimmy!" Luke exclaimed, out of breath.

It had been three years since Luke had bolted down the stairs of Jimmy's old apartment, but he looked the same.

"What are you doing here?" Jimmy asked.

"I thought it was you," Luke proclaimed. "I thought I saw you last week going into your class, but I wasn't sure if it really was you or not."

"It's me."

A pregnant pause lingered between the two, uncomfortably waiting to be filled. Jimmy struggled to stay calm despite the familiar knot forming in his stomach. There was so much he wanted to say, so many questions. He had hoped for so long to finally gain some answers, to learn where he'd gone wrong, to find out why he wasn't good enough. But now, all that remained was that unsettled feeling of sickness, a gut-wrenching tug at his insides.

"I'm taking a class down the hall." Luke said, pointing behind him where a small group of students emerged, holding large art boards and sketchpads. "We meet twice a week. I think it's the same schedule as yours."

Jimmy's breath shortened. His heart raced. He silently reprimanded himself for getting nervous or anxious or feeling anything at all. It was an affront to his self-respect to still desire a boy who wanted nothing to do with him.

"Small world," Jimmy said. "What's the class?"

"Figure drawing," Luke replied, lowering his head as though embarrassed by the truth. "I don't think I'm an artist or anything, just thought it could help with my work to get a little refresher."

"That's great. And how are you? Everything good?" Jimmy asked, attempting to mask his discomfort with friendliness.

"I'm good. Everything's good. And you?"

A few of the art students made their way down the narrow hallway, approaching Jimmy and Luke. Jimmy moved a few steps to his right as the group passed, carrying their cumbersome supplies. Luke followed, focus glued to Jimmy. Silence returned once the students had passed. Luke fumbled with his frayed sketchbook, shifting it around as if in search of some activity to distract from the moment's awkwardness.

Jimmy peered down, spotting Luke's Converses, likely the same sneakers from three years ago, now covered in a thick layer of wear and tear. Luke's dirty sneakers, the raggedy sketchpad, his shirt still one size too big—it all added up to the same adorable boy Jimmy had so quickly fallen for years ago.

"Sorry, but I should get going," Jimmy announced. "It's late and I've got a commute. But it was good to see you again."

"James," Luke interjected as he reached over, taking hold of Jimmy's hand. "Do you have a minute?" Luke retracted, letting go of Jimmy's fingers as if realizing he had overstepped. "Can we talk?" His voice quivered with tenderness.

Jimmy hesitated, fighting against what he knew he wanted. "I really can't right now," he replied. "I'm sorry. I still have work to do and it's already pretty late."

Luke's face fell and his chest caved in, his eager intent seemingly crushed. Jimmy's resolve softened. Despite his best efforts, he had never managed to forget that tiny something that existed between them. Life's ceaseless momentum had swept the actual taste of it back to that place where nearly forgotten memories live, but the familiar surge of joy he felt in Luke's presence was unshakeable. There was no denying his excitement, even if he knew better.

"I got kinda nervous when I spotted you last month," Luke admitted.

"Last month?"

"But I didn't know if it was you or I was just imagining you," Luke continued. "Now whenever I come to class, I get worried I might run into you, but then I don't see you and I feel disappointed." His lush eyebrows came together, the narrow bridge of bareness between them shortening. His face seemed fuller now. He had put on weight, but it did him well. The hazy brown hue of his eyes shimmered with sincerity. He was even more handsome than Jimmy remembered.

"I was thinking of grabbing a taco from the truck down the street. Are you hungry?" Jimmy asked.

Luke's face lit up.

Jimmy listened while Luke rambled on about his new job as they made their way across the street. Jimmy didn't mind. He enjoyed the excitement in Luke's voice. He was working as an illustrator, freelancing on projects in order to build his portfolio. He had done well enough to quit his part-time job and move out of Jersey. Jimmy was pleased to hear of Luke's success. There were times when he had imagined otherwise, hoping Luke might still be stuck in his mom's basement in Jersey making subs and cleaning tables, but truthfully he had always hoped Luke was doing well.

Jimmy ordered the tacos, refusing Luke's offer to pay, and they took a seat on the cold concrete surround of a nearby water fountain. Luke took a timidly small bite of the sweltering hot taco meat while Jimmy waited for his to cool.

"Holy shit that's hot," Luke said, mouth wide open.

Jimmy chuckled. "It just got off the grill. Give it some time."

Jimmy blew on his taco for some time before taking a bite. Tiny drops of fountain water flew through the cold air and landed on the back of his neck. Hot and spicy, the taco warmed his chilled body.

"My mouth is on fire," Luke announced, his eyes watering.

Jimmy spotted Luke's empty bottle of water in his lap. "Here, we can share," he said, passing his bottle to Luke.

Jimmy watched from the corner of his eye as Luke's lips took to his bottle of water. Luke was careful to take small sips, taking breaks in between like an out-of-breath athlete. Jimmy's pounding heart had quieted. The silence that fell between them now felt easy, welcome even. Moments passed without much of a word, but the tension had so quickly lifted. Luke drew circles in the air with his foot dangling above the pavement as they sat perched on the concrete wall. Jimmy wanted to be mad at him, to reprimand the adorable stranger in some way for so easily discarding him years ago. But the peaceful stillness he now felt could not be agitated.

"I can't believe it's been so long since I last saw you," Luke said.

Jimmy pretended to think, as if he hadn't done the math every time he remembered Luke. Time had a way of being elusive, seemingly insignificant moments getting lost in a haze of triviality, but certain moments stood as landmarks, pillars of happiness or sorrow or lost hope that marked the path. Luke was one of those landmarks, boldly etched in Jimmy's timeline, incapable of being removed. He would never really be able to forget how long it had been.

"Three years, I think."

"Three years," Luke repeated in a solemn tone.

Luke then apologized for hogging the conversation and asked about Jimmy. He inquired about Jimmy's job and friends, trying to make sense of the gap in their timeline with bits and pieces of Jimmy's stories. A powerful desire crept up inside Jimmy, a longing to share pieces of himself he had kept locked away. He wished, in that moment, they could be friends so that he might be able to speak freely. He longed to tell Luke how much he missed having Charlie around, how lonely he sometimes felt. He even longed to tell him about the few failed attempts at romance that had filled the past three years with rejuvenated hope and familiar disappointment. He yearned to admit that he had, in some involuntary way, lost the hope that once fueled his resolve. But he knew he could not. Time and experience had done its work. Jimmy had grown protective of himself, not easily trusting of others, jaded even.

Luke listened, his attention unwavering but his eyes soft and caring. Jimmy looked away, growing more and more uncomfortable, but Luke probed him further—one thoughtful, motivated question after another. It was impossible for him to hide from the sharp light cast on him as Luke attempted to peer beneath the surface.

"You've changed," Luke interjected, his words laced with the slightest hint of disappointment.

"I guess I grew up," Jimmy replied. He sprang up from the concrete seat, wiping the sides of his mouth as he made his way to the trash can.

Luke hurried to finish the last bit of taco left and joined Jimmy.

"You know what I could really use?" Luke asked, his mouth still full. "A coffee." He finished chewing and smiled cunningly, awaiting a response.

His real-life grin far exceeded the imagined one in Jimmy's memories. Jimmy's body filled with warmth at the sight of it. He thought about putting a stop to it all, ending the evening while he was ahead, but the part of him that wanted to stay commanded attention.

"There's a place a couple blocks from here," Jimmy offered. "I've never tried their coffee before, but it would give me an excuse for dessert."

Luke's face lit up, his porcelain skin shining extra brightly as they made their way downtown, walking like old friends with an uninterrupted history.

"So, how is life outside of work and tacos?" Luke asked. He had grown giddy, a subtle skip now in his step.

"Good. Though there isn't much life outside of work and tacos," Jimmy replied as he tugged at his jacket zipper, hoping to find more length. "Can I see some of your sketches?" He pointed to the notebook nestled under Luke's arm.

"No," Luke replied. "Definitely not."

"Come on. Why not?"

"It's all shit." Luke shook his head.

"Oh, please. I'm sure it's great."

"Honestly, I'm not trying to be modest." The faintest shade of pink washed over Luke's face. "Sorry to be weird about it, but I've seen your drawings, remember?"

Jimmy was surprised to find that he had forgotten that small detail of their brief history together, certain he had retained it all with precise clarity. It came rushing back to him. Luke had stumbled on a sketchbook hanging out of Jimmy's bag while on the train together. Jimmy was in and out of a nap, unaware that Luke had reached in and taken it. When he discovered Luke thumbing through his most private work, Jimmy sprang into action, punching his boney shoulder with more force than he had intended. Luke cried out in pain and returned the book to its rightful place.

"Well then, it's only fair I see yours," Jimmy demanded, but Luke was unwavering. He fumbled with the sketchbook, tucking it snuggly under his arm to keep it out of sight. Jimmy surrendered. He had no desire to make anyone uncomfortable, least of all Luke.

"You intimidate me sometimes," Luke admitted with another near whisper.

Jimmy swung his body around to face Luke, shuffling sideways along the sidewalk, staring with confusion at Luke while waiting for him to continue.

Luke's crooked smile grew, his attention fixed straight ahead.

Jimmy cleared his throat, hoping to motivate a response, but Luke remained quiet, his lopsided grin frozen on his glowing face. Jimmy had never intimidated anyone before, at least not knowingly.

When they arrived at the café, the shop was nearly empty, closing time fast approaching. Luke studied the chalkboard menu hanging behind the counter.

"Doesn't look like they have any of your froufrou, artisanal, pour-over bullshit," he said as he reached over, grabbing Jimmy by the shoulders. "Are you going to manage with just a regular drip?" He squeezed, his hands knowingly massaging the tense area, their warmth penetrating the layers of wool and fleece, the delicate force of his fingers and thumbs reaching Jimmy's bare flesh. Jimmy's breath shortened.

"I guess I have no choice. It'll have to do," Jimmy responded as he pulled away, unable to bear the heat any longer. He bent over the display of day-old pastries and desserts, pretending to study his options while quieting his mind. "And since you're buying, maybe one of these chocolate chunk brownies."

They sat at a table near the window, the city at their side fading into the first hours of night. Luke's lips puckered as he blew carefully over the hot liquid. The steaming-hot taco had taught him a lesson. A light mist of steam rose up, slightly blurring his face from view. His slender fingers held the coffee near, nails surprisingly more manicured, edges no longer rough and jagged. His hands still possessed that feminine elegance, long and thin. He moved them carefully, though unaware of their allure.

Luke looked up from behind the steam, his gaze connecting with Jimmy's. "So, what do you think?"

"About what?" Jimmy asked.

"The coffee. Any good?"

Jimmy swirled the cup around like a glass of wine and took a petite sip, allowing the warm beverage to rest in his mouth for some time. "Eh, I've had worse."

"You look good," Luke noted. "I like your hair this way. More natural."

"Thanks. I can't take credit for it, though, merely a lack of time and patience." Jimmy smiled uncomfortably. "You look good too. Different, but good."

"I gained weight."

"You did." Jimmy chuckled. "A little. I like it, though. Looks good on you."

"Are you seeing anyone?" Luke asked, his face deliberately aimed down toward his cup.

Jimmy shuddered. He thought of stories to tell, versions of the truth that might cast him in a better light, stories that didn't end with him defeated. But the undeniable familiarity he felt with Luke quashed his desire to lie, so he brought up Chris.

"We met not long after me and you," Jimmy recalled. "It was nothing, really—now that I look back at it. But at the time, it felt like something."

Chris was nothing more than a sexual escapade that went on for far too long, but Jimmy had no desire to relive his sexual awakening, not when a far more significant part of his past was sitting right in front of him.

"What about you?" Jimmy asked. "Are you seeing anyone?"

"No. Not currently," Luke replied, his body noticeably tightening. "I was. It wasn't serious and it didn't last very long."

Jimmy sank into his chair. The thought of Luke with someone else made his body heavy, though he knew he could claim no ownership. Luke was never his. Jimmy knew that all too well. But defeat came rushing back, nonetheless.

"I learned a lot, I think," Luke continued. "But we never really clicked. It just felt so forced, like we both wanted a relationship bad enough to try and make it work even though it was obvious we barely liked each other."

Jimmy squirmed, trying to appear comfortable as he nodded in support.

"It wasn't nearly as easy as it was with us," Luke added. "At first, I was just going along with it because I thought I should. Like it was good for me in some way or I needed the experience. But now I see how stupid that is."

Jimmy froze at the thought of Luke comparing him to another unknown lover. He hadn't imagined Luke might consider what they had *easy*. It had been easy. It still was. Jimmy, of course, recognized that from the onset, but it was surprising to hear Luke knew it as well. A rush of joy and relief and confusion came crashing down.

"I know what you mean," Jimmy replied, unwilling to take the bait if there even was bait to take. "It sometimes seems like more work than it's worth."

Luke grinned halfheartedly as he peered into his nearly empty cup, suddenly saddened. Jimmy watched him for a moment, desperately wanting to liven his mood, to reinvigorate his crooked smile, to feel his soft skin pressed once more against his own. But any more time spent with Luke was dangerous.

"It's getting late," Jimmy said. "I should probably get going."

"But you barely touched your coffee."

"It was really only good for a few sips."

"Where are you heading? Can I walk with you?" Luke asked.

Jimmy hesitated, wanting to save himself from potentially reliving another disaster, but he couldn't resist. "I have to catch the F. There's a stop a couple blocks from here."

The heat underground provided a welcome change from the chill above. Luke removed his thin jacket as they stood near the tracks, alone in the desolate station, the usual throng of daily commuters already nestled away safely in their homes.

"I have to admit I'm happy to have some company. I never like taking the train this late," Jimmy noted.

"I don't blame you." Luke gestured to a lonely straggler approaching, the ends of his dirt-crusted pants sweeping the filthy pavement.

"I don't need a damn one of you!" the straggler shouted, turning to face Jimmy and Luke as he passed. "Jesus is my only true friend! My savior! He will punish the sinners! Damn them all to hell! Let them burn for all eternity!"

Jimmy raised his head to the man who vanished in the distance and braced back on the steel pillar behind him with an amused smile that turned into a yawn.

"Jesus's buddy," he said to Luke.

"Who knew? Right here in New York."

Luke's hands were pressed firmly in his pockets, his jacket nestled under his arm as he stood near the pillar across from Jimmy.

"He could use a shower, though," Jimmy added, wincing at the lingering stench.

Luke chuckled and moved closer, peering down to the ground. "So you like it in Astoria?"

"I do. A lot actually. I really feel like I found my spot."

Luke continued his approach as his voice quieted further. "That's a nice feeling."

Jimmy's focus remained fixed, unable to look away as Luke stepped closer and closer. He opened himself to Luke's approach, the space between his legs uncontrollably widening.

"How did you end up in Midtown?" Jimmy asked, struggling to breathe normally as the distance between the two vanished.

Luke slid into the space between Jimmy's legs, coming to a slow and deliberate stop once the gap between their bodies was almost entirely closed.

"What's wrong with Midtown?" Luke asked.

Their voices were now whispers.

"No one of worth lives in Midtown," Jimmy replied.

Luke grabbed the dangling flap of Jimmy's jacket pocket, lightly tugging at it. "*I* live in Midtown," he whispered.

"Exactly. Looks like you found your spot too."

"Ouch," Luke quietly exclaimed. His face was only inches away, the microscopic heaviness of his dark eyelashes now clearly visible.

Jimmy's heart raced, but his attention remained bravely fixed. He inhaled, catching his breath as Luke leaned in to graze the tip of his nose against Jimmy's, artfully testing the waters, waiting for a reaction. Jimmy's gaze fell on Luke's lips. Their mouths opened, stilted breathing harmonizing. Jimmy's eyelids fell when their lips finally met, tentatively at first—small, moist pecks as they reacquainted themselves with familiar terrain. Luke's warm touch traveled up Jimmy's torso, landing at the back of his neck as their mouths opened more readily, their lips now fully in flight. Jimmy's body surrendered as Luke pressed forward, pushing him farther against the cold, steel pillar. Jimmy grabbed on to Luke's face, holding it firmly in his grasp as their tongues caressed. His taste was the same, his breath just as familiar. Their bodies joined together like pieces of the same puzzle, well-acquainted companions with an everyday familiarity. They pulled and tugged knowingly.

When their mouths grew tired, they separated. Luke rested his forehead against Jimmy's as their breathing returned to normalcy. Jimmy peered down to the dirty sneakers nestled close to his brown leather dress shoes, having aptly found their spot. He smiled at the happy union, though the tiniest ping of worry emerged. His teeth clenched together as he swallowed hard, peeling himself away just as the low and faint bass of an approaching train echoed through the underground passage, ominous lights charging forward from the horizon.

"That's my train," Jimmy whispered.

"When can I see you again?" Luke asked.

"You still have my number?"

Chapter Five

"WOW. IT'S BIG," Luke said, wide-eyed. "Really big."

"Well, thanks," Jimmy replied as he emerged from the bathroom, zipping up his pants.

"A one-bedroom this size is pretty impressive," Luke added.

"You get more for your money in Queens."

They had spent most of the pleasantly warm Saturday together. Day faded into night as the happily reunited friends had strolled the streets of Jimmy's quaint neighborhood, eating ice cream in the nearby park, sifting through old books and used clothing at the local thrift shop, catching up on lost time. Hours passed with ease as the sun had quickly set and stores closed their doors for the day. It hadn't been until Jimmy entered his apartment that the ease seemed to dissipate. He had been free of his mind's relentless thrashing all day, but the clamor returned once the two were locked away, alone together, the present too eerily reminiscent of an ill-fated past.

"So happy to finally be relieved," Jimmy said as he made his way to the tight, galley kitchen. "Can I get you something to drink? I don't have much in the way of alcohol but beer and a little gin."

"A beer would be great."

Luke sat on Jimmy's couch, already at home when Jimmy approached, handing him the cold, wet bottle. Their hands met for a moment in the exchange.

Jimmy took a seat on the couch, making sure to leave an ample amount of space between him and his visitor. He pressed his thumb into the cold beer bottle as he commanded his leg to cease from bobbing up and down.

Luke's gaze wandered around the living room, scanning and surveying every detail. "James, your place really is something."

"Really? What do you mean?"

"It's a home. Not just an apartment."

Jimmy was flattered to find his hard work had been recognized by none other than a boy he so desired. He explained how excited he had been to find the place, how adultlike the whole thing had made him feel. He was eager to share stories about the work he had done, how the landlord had allowed him to sand and refinish parts of the floor himself. He'd painted the walls carefully chosen shades of gray, accenting the space with pops of color here and there. Most of his finds came from thrift stores and flea markets, bargains he was proud to display. His parents had been worried about him moving to Queens, but their ill-conceived perception of the neighborhood changed once they'd visited.

"So are you not gonna give me a tour?" Luke asked.

"This is it," Jimmy replied as he looked around. "You've seen it all. Except for the bedroom."

"Exactly."

Jimmy smiled, unable to mask his bashfulness. "You've gotta earn that right, my friend."

"Oh, really?" Luke asked as he placed his beer bottle on the coffee table and scooched closer. "And what do I need to do to earn that right?"

"I don't know where you think you're going," Jimmy said as the smile grew brighter. "This is not what I had in mind when I invited you up here."

Luke continued his approach until the space between them vanished. His comforting, puffy eyes remained fixed. His hand fell with ease onto Jimmy's thigh. He squeezed it tenderly.

"So what did you have in mind?" he whispered.

"Look, we're just two friends having a beer," Jimmy replied, trying to hide the delight etched on his face.

"Right. Of course. Just friends having a beer."

Luke pried the bottle from Jimmy's hand and rested it on the table near his. Jimmy allowed it, no longer able to pretend he didn't want what was coming.

Their lips met more urgently this time, coming together like magnets in close proximity. Jimmy lunged forward, pinning Luke down on the other end of the couch as he bit gently at his visitor's bottom lip. An entire day of stolen glances had filled him with an unquenchable thirst. Luke tugged at strands of Jimmy's hair, moaning in satisfaction as he fought back. Jimmy drew the tip of his tongue along the contours of Luke's face, paying careful attention to every region of his silky, smooth skin. Luke wrapped his legs around, opening himself to Jimmy who thrust his pelvis forward. Their bodies grinded together, gaining momentum. Back and forth, they swayed.

"Wait, wait," Luke finally whispered, already on the verge of climaxing.

Jimmy pushed harder, grinding their clothed crotches together with greater speed. Luke's mouth opened wide, his teeth grazing against Jimmy's cheek as he painfully cried out with pleasure. He grabbed on tightly, holding Jimmy close as he finished. Jimmy snickered, allowing his body to stay nestled close as Luke kissed his cheek and chin and neck.

"What?" Luke asked with an exhausted grin.

"That was quick." Jimmy pried himself off Luke and rose to his knees, still straddling Luke as he adjusted his shirt and hair.

"Come back," Luke whispered, tugging at Jimmy's shirt.

Jimmy took Luke's hand and interlocked fingers as he sat comfortably on Luke's thighs. He had wanted to take Luke's hand in his own all day as they walked along sidewalks and in and out of shops. He took pleasure in possessing it for a moment. They made a handsome pair, the two hands.

Luke's thumb traveled around Jimmy's fingers, feeling their curves and edges. He stared at Jimmy, breathing slow and heavy.

"I don't think friends dry hump," Jimmy said, that sting of worry and concern returning again.

"Says who? I do this with all my friends."

"I bet you do." Jimmy stared back at Luke who was smiling brightly. His head rested awkwardly against the hard edge of the sofa. Jimmy reached behind, grabbed a pillow, and placed it under Luke's head. "I think this was maybe not the best idea."

"Do you want me to go?" Luke asked.

"No. That's kinda the problem," Jimmy replied, flattening Luke's wrinkled shirt. "But I think maybe you should."

Luke lifted himself up slowly until face-to-face with Jimmy. "But you don't want me to," he whispered. He hovered with his lips deviously close to Jimmy's, teasing them with proximity but not allowing them to touch.

Jimmy's gaze fell as he rested his hand against Luke's. "What are we doing exactly?"

"Picking up where we left off," Luke replied.

Jimmy stared down at Luke's gleaming teeth. His grin worked with skillful diligence, wielding a familiar power over Jimmy. Luke was not just anyone, not some random encounter to enjoy in the moment. He knew going further would only make things harder. He would never really be able to be casual with Luke the way he had been with other men. He pulled his face away, peeled himself off the sofa, and peered down at Luke as he rose to his feet.

"You should go," he said tenderly. He lifted the beers from the table, trying to occupy himself with some activity. "This was fun, but it's late."

Luke pulled his legs inward, sitting upright in attention as he grabbed the beers away from Jimmy and placed them back on the table. He took hold of Jimmy's hips and guided him back to the couch. Jimmy allowed himself to be commanded until he was once again seated near Luke, his attempt to get away thwarted.

"Oh, shit. I'm sorry," Luke apologized, remembering his sneakers. "I should've taken them off. Don't want to mess up your couch."

Jimmy smiled. "It doesn't matter."

"I remember you were particular about not wearing shoes in the house," Luke noted as he freed his legs.

"I wouldn't say I'm particular about it. It's not like a rule or anything. I have mine on."

Luke removed his sneakers and placed them neatly under the sofa. Jimmy chuckled, taking notice of his maroon-and-yellow striped socks.

"What?" Luke asked.

"Your socks."

"You don't like my socks?" Luke raised his legs, displaying his stripped feet to the audience of two.

"They look like Harry Potter's scarf."

Luke laughed, seeing the socks in a new light. "You're right. They do, don't they?"

"They're, oddly enough, the kind of socks I would buy."

"Well, let me see yours."

Jimmy chucked his sneakers, revealing his plaid socks covered in varied shades of pink and blue. He raised his feet to meet Luke's. "See—just as crazy, but not nearly as cool."

"I busted these out just for you."

Jimmy chuckled, his mood lighter. "Lucky me."

"I thought I might impress you with my notable fashion sense."

"Well, job well done. I definitely took notice. Did you go out and buy these just for the occasion?"

"No."

Jimmy glared in disbelief.

"Okay, okay—maybe," Luke admitted. "I picked these up the other day. Not exclusively for this but I won't lie, the thought crossed my mind. The last time I was at your house, I felt gross, like my socks were too frumpy and dirty. I always worried I stank."

Jimmy laughed at the ridiculousness of Luke's concern. He had never seen anything about Luke as anything other than endearing.

"I can assure you I don't remember your dirty socks," Jimmy replied. "I had bigger things on my mind that night."

Luke's smile faded. His expression grew pensive. The day had been filled with lightheartedness, but the elephant in the room remained, whether ignored or otherwise.

"I'm sorry," Luke said, shifting. "About that night and about disappearing afterward. I was shitty to you."

Jimmy looked away. "It doesn't matter. It was a long time ago."

"No, it does matter." Luke adjusted himself, sitting cross-legged again to aim his body toward Jimmy. "I was such an idiot."

"You don't owe me anything," Jimmy replied. "It's not like we were dating. We barely knew each other."

"That's not how I saw it."

"How did you see it?"

"I really liked you."

"Did you?" Jimmy asked sharply.

"Of course I did. You know that."

"I thought I did, but what was I supposed to think?" Jimmy could feel a burst of heat fill his body, but he quieted the surge, not wanting to lose his cool. "Things were going so well until they weren't."

Luke's head fell in defeat.

"I tried," Jimmy continued. "I called. I reached out. But you didn't want anything to do with me. Eventually I just accepted that I imagined the whole thing and we were never really on the same page."

"I don't know how to describe it," Luke replied, still gazing down. "I've gone over it in my head so many times, but it still doesn't make much sense. I was so confused about so many things. And then I got back from Boston and didn't know how to deal with it all or what to do. So I just did nothing and ignored you. Like an asshole."

Jimmy grew more and more uncomfortable as Luke continued, fearful to uncover the truth. There was, however, the slightest bit of relief in knowing that their time together hadn't been completely dismissed. It held weight for Luke as it always had for Jimmy.

"For so long after that night, I cursed myself for that fucking cheese platter," Jimmy admitted.

"Cheese platter?"

"You don't remember? I had a whole setup: cheese and crackers and wine. So lame. It just sat there on my coffee table after you left, laughing at me."

Luke chuckled. "It had nothing to do with the cheese platter."

"I kept thinking I should have gone with beer and chips instead. Maybe then you would've stuck around."

Luke laughed again, this time burying his face in his hands for a moment. "Oh, man. James. I am so sorry."

"It's not like I pictured us riding off into the sunset together, but I really liked you. All I wanted was a chance to see where things might go. But you just up and left. Literally. You sprang up like my couch was on fire."

"I know. I know. I was an idiot. I got scared. I don't know, maybe it *was* your cheese platter."

"I knew it!"

"It was everything. I felt so un-gay around you, like there was something wrong with me."

"*Un-gay?* What does that even mean?"

"You were always perfectly put together, with your perfectly decorated apartment and your fancy job. And— well, your cheese platter. I worked at a fucking sub shop in Jersey!"

Jimmy listened as Luke described what he had been going through, how he was unsure of whom he should be and what he wanted.

"I had just come out and was already feeling out of place," he said. "I liked you. I knew I liked you from the very beginning, but then I started feeling bad about myself whenever I was around you. Questioning everything, like I wasn't good enough or we were just too different. It actually made me mad at you, I think. I decided I needed someone more like me."

Jimmy nodded, encouraging Luke to continue despite how uncomfortable the confession was making him.

"I think I got scared," Luke continued, "because I could tell it was the kind of thing that was going to get serious fast and—I guess, on some level, I didn't know if I could handle it. So I convinced myself I didn't want to be with you, that we weren't right for each other. It was the easiest thing to do."

Jimmy had, over the years, invented many reasons for Luke fleeing, made-up versions of the truth that helped appease his troubled mind. The most logical of them being that they were too different. He had managed to convince himself that it would never have ended well even if they had given it a try because their worlds were so far apart. They were, in fact, different. Jimmy knew it even when his emotions were at their highest, but that incontestable nearness they shared seemed to overpower any sense of reason that would have otherwise served him well.

"We are different," Jimmy admitted. "You weren't wrong."

"No! That's my point," Luke exclaimed. "I *was* wrong. None of those things matter. It was stupid to ever think they did."

"Don't they, though?" Jimmy asked, unconvinced. He sighed as he sank deep into the couch, surrendering to his confusion. He wanted to believe Luke, to focus only on how good it felt to be near him, how strongly the knot in his stomach fastened at the mere sight of his smile, but there was more to the equation. He understood that now.

Luke waited patiently for Jimmy to offer a verdict. "Do you want me to leave?"

"No," Jimmy replied.

Luke shrugged, accepting the answer. He threw himself down onto the couch and extended his legs out as he reclined, stretching his body across the length of the tiny sofa. His feet landed snuggly in Jimmy's lap as he made himself comfortable.

Jimmy couldn't help but smile. He rested his hands on the maroon-and-yellow striped socks now in his possession. "So, what? You're just gonna stick around?"

"Oh, yeah. I'm not going anywhere." Luke gleamed with contentment as he threw his hands behind his head.

"They do stink a little," Jimmy said with a pretend grimace as he tugged at the socks.

"Fuck off. No they don't."

"Move over," Jimmy demanded as he maneuvered his way around Luke's lanky body. He landed in the space near Luke, rested his head on the shared pillow, and stared up toward the ceiling. Luke's shoulder jabbed into his own.

"You're so fucking boney," Jimmy exclaimed, pushing Luke's shoulder out of the way.

"You're gonna throw me off the couch!" Luke shouted. He turned to his side, facing Jimmy as he clasped his hands and rested them near his cheek. "Better?"

"It'll have to do."

"Not my fault your couch is so small."

Jimmy's attention moved from the ceiling to Luke, who nestled closer, looking like a little boy at bedtime. He took Luke's hand and examined it more closely. He ran his thumb along the edges of his fingernails.

"You stopped biting your nails."

"I did," Luke concurred, seemingly gleeful Jimmy had noticed.

Jimmy placed Luke's hand on his chest. It rested there, rising and falling along with Jimmy's breathing as his eyes gradually shut. Luke's eyes also closed. His breathing grew quieter, all remaining tension vanishing until they both surrendered to sleep.

Jimmy awoke, hours later, in the middle of the night. He peeled his head from the pillow, sat up, and dug for his phone. Luke was fast asleep.

"Luke," Jimmy whispered as he lightly shook his shoulder.

Luke's eyes struggled to open. He squinted in Jimmy's direction.

"Let's go to bed," Jimmy suggested groggily.

Luke nodded in agreement, too tired to find words. Jimmy pulled him from the couch and ushered him to the bedroom where they fell onto the mattress with ease. Their foreheads touched as they lay on their sides, facing each other, eyes lightly sealed.

They kissed softly, still half-asleep.

"Is it okay if we just sleep?" Luke asked.

"Of course," Jimmy whispered. He flipped to rest on his other side, pushing his back close to Luke who wrapped his arms knowingly around Jimmy, holding him near.

"I made it into the bedroom," Luke whispered into Jimmy's ear in a low grumble. "Guess I earned the right."

Jimmy smiled, his body tingling. "I guess so."

Chapter Six

SUNLIGHT POURED ONTO the bed from the corner window. The neighboring building's harsh yellow walls cast a golden hue over the room. Jimmy awoke to its glare nearly singeing the skin on his forehead. He freed himself from Luke and rested on his back. The events of the day before fired off in Jimmy's mind, sweeping over him like a deck of playing cards rapidly shuffled until they landed here, waking up with Luke in his bed. Luke was fast asleep, his mouth slightly ajar. He seemed completely at ease, unaware of the foreign surroundings or Jimmy's fixed gaze—at home, as if it was just one of many mornings spent in Jimmy's bed.

Jimmy studied his boyish face, appreciating every feature. His lips were dry, the faintest layer of crust barely discernible along the edges. His eyes were softly sealed, the darkness of his eyelids a stark contrast to his light skin. Luke was his to enjoy as he pleased, at least for now. He longed to squeeze him so tightly it hurt, to wrap his arms around him and breathe him in. Instead, he settled for examining Luke, making mental note of exactly how he looked in that moment, storing it away so that he might have a more vivid image of him to conjure up should he run off again.

Luke reached over, eyes still sealed, and wrapped his arm across Jimmy's chest. He pulled himself closer. Jimmy opened his arms to make room as Luke comfortably rested his head on Jimmy's shoulder.

Jimmy smiled freely, aware that his satisfaction couldn't be seen as he looked down at Luke. He allowed his hand to fall onto the shaggy nest of curls that lay in front of him. His fingers weaved in and out of locks of hair as Luke buried his face farther into Jimmy, sighing peacefully.

Worry seeped in as Jimmy delighted in holding Luke. Getting too comfortable too quickly was dangerous.

"Should we have breakfast?" Jimmy whispered.

Luke's eyes fluttered open. He ran his hand across Jimmy's chest as he moaned like an unhappy child not wanting to go to school. His touch made its way down to Jimmy's stomach. His eyes grew less weary as he reached into Jimmy's shirt and allowed his hand to rest on bare skin.

Heat traveled through Jimmy like an electric charge. The warmth of Luke's hand resting on his stomach caused his blood to travel south.

Luke teetered back and forth, falling asleep, and then waking up again until he finally took a deep breath as if to force himself to stay alert.

"Why is it so bright in here?" he asked, squinting.

He kissed Jimmy's neck and chin, working his way to his lips, where he pecked before opening his mouth. Jimmy's lips parted. Luke's morning taste was sharp, but intoxicating. Jimmy breathed it in as his erection grew.

Luke's leg grazed against Jimmy's crotch, back and forth, before he mounted him, laying his weight on top of him as his hand moved down. He unbuttoned Jimmy's jeans, sneaked inside, and grabbed his erect penis with a devious smile.

"Good morning."

Jimmy chuckled as he willingly surrendered to Luke's touch. Luke ran his hand up and down, gently grazing the tip, working his way down the shaft with care. Jimmy's eyes rolled back as he sighed quietly. Luke scaled down Jimmy as he continued stroking, dropping to Jimmy's hips where he carefully pulled Jimmy's jeans down and peeled off his boxers. Jimmy winced as Luke's mouth wrapped around his sensitive flesh. His body shuddered. Luke bobbed up and down, wetness gliding across Jimmy's bare and tender skin. Jimmy clenched the pillow behind him as Luke devoured him, his hand and mouth working in unison with growing intensity until Jimmy could no longer contain his arousal. It burst forward with a cry of relief.

Luke held Jimmy's throbbing shaft, squeezing the tip as it pulsated so as to drain it completely. Jimmy's body twitched in pain until he could no longer bear it. He grasped Luke's face and guided him away. Luke examined his wet fingers for a moment, covered in the sticky cream, before licking them clean like a hungry cat.

Jimmy watched, wide-eyed and amused. "You're a freak."

"Only with you, buddy."

THE SMALL AND less-than-immaculate Greek café was not Jimmy's first choice, but Luke insisted it was good enough. Sunday brunch was in full swing, and even in Queens, it was hard to get a table anywhere else. It had proven sufficient enough until their meals came out, cold and tasting stale.

"This toast is at least a day or two old," Jimmy complained as he waved the slice of rubbery bread in the air.

"No it's not. Let me see." Luke leaned in and struggled to pry a bite from the tough slice. "Okay. Maybe you're right."

"The eggs are also cold," Jimmy added.

"Will you stop complaining!" Luke took a bite of his omelet. He chewed carefully, masking his grimace with a forced smile that he directed at Jimmy.

"You know it's awful."

"It's not the best I've ever had," Luke admitted as he struggled to swallow. "But it's not so bad."

"We should have waited at the last place."

"Did you really want to wait in that line?"

"No," Jimmy replied, "but their cake donut-things are amazing."

"Who needs a cake donut? I got my dose of sweet goodness this morning," Luke replied as he slurped his finger.

Jimmy glared, holding back a smile.

"My fingers still smell of it," Luke proclaimed as he waved his hand in front of Jimmy who smacked it away.

"Finish your cold omelet so we can get out of here."

Jimmy washed down the final bite of stale bread with a gulp of bitter coffee. Luke continued tentatively with his meal, poking at it until finally giving up. He dropped his fork in defeat and leaned back in the cold metal chair, stretching his legs out as he reclined. They landed comfortably between Jimmy's. Their feet rested side by side as they finished their coffee.

"What do you have going on today?" Luke asked.

"Nothing much, just usual Sunday errands. You?"

"No plans. Want to spend the day together?"

Jimmy's face tightened as he deliberated over it. "Eh—"

Luke kicked Jimmy's chair, nudging Jimmy backward.

"Okay. Fine," Jimmy agreed. "Why not? It is a beautiful day out. Let's roam around the city and soak up the sun."

They had no agenda in mind as they waited for the train. Luke inched close to the edge of the platform, hung one foot over, and pretended to lose his balance.

"You're an idiot," Jimmy said as he looked away.

"Would you save me if I fell over?"

"You deserve to fall over. Stop messing around. You know how many people actually do fall over?"

Luke shook his head as he waited for the answer.

"Well, I don't actually know—but I'm sure a lot do."

Luke pulled his leg in and backed away from the yellow line at the platform's edge. "All right, I'll stop," he said as he approached Jimmy. "I'm making you nervous."

"I'm not nervous. It's your life you're risking, not mine."

"Come on, you know if I fell, you'd jump in there all hysterical and shit."

Jimmy smiled as he imagined himself screaming while trying to save Luke. Luke approached, laughing, and pressed his forehead to Jimmy's as the train approached.

He let out an exaggerated sigh of relief as he geared his attention to the stopping train. "Barely moved out of the way in time."

The train was nearly empty when they entered. They took seats side by side and watched out the dirty window as the station zipped by.

"I have to admit," Luke said, "Queens is nicer than I thought it would be."

"Was this your first time in Queens?" Jimmy asked, stunned.

"I think so."

Jimmy sighed, shaking his head in disbelief.

"What? What reason would I have to come out here? I don't even go to Brooklyn much unless I have to."

"*Brooklyn*," Jimmy said with disgust. "I'm so sick of Brooklyn."

"Fucking hipsters."

"It's overrated and now overpriced, and for what?"

"I'm actually surprised you're not a bigger fan," Luke noted. "Seems like your kind of scene."

"What's that supposed to mean?" Jimmy asked as he turned to face him.

"Everyone is cool and on trend and everything is handmade and organic," Luke replied jeeringly. "Also all the hipster coffee—seems like you'd be in heaven."

"I do appreciate the coffee," Jimmy admitted. "It's hard to find good coffee in my neighborhood."

"Yeah, Brooklyn's all about pour-over."

Jimmy smiled as he rolled his eyes, reprimanding himself for being so amused. He had, in truth, loved Brooklyn at first. It was where he'd met Charlie, where he had spent most of his weekends, eating and drinking in Williamsburg and Greenpoint, partying in Bushwick and Gowanus. But in time, the allure of that scene faded and he sought an escape from the same bars and people, all perfectly unkempt with their statement beards and torn-up jeans, sheltered and protected from the rest of New York. Astoria became his getaway, his home away from it all where real life still seemed to prevail.

"Did Chris live in Queens?" Luke asked.

Jimmy's eyes widened. He had almost forgotten he'd mentioned Chris.

"No. Brooklyn."

Luke nodded, seemingly happy the ex-lover was from a borough Jimmy now detested.

"And you guys were dating for how long?"

"I wouldn't exactly say we were dating," Jimmy replied as he adjusted his position on the hard subway seat. Earlier, when he'd felt that overwhelming need to protect himself, he had shied away from divulging any details, but things were already different. The wall had crumbled. He no longer felt the need to hide his past.

Luke grew more inquisitive as Jimmy described how he'd met Chris and the nature of their time together. It had been obvious early on that Jimmy and Chris weren't right for each other, but their bodies had their own agenda, uncontrollably clinging to each other. The force of that push and pull had been intoxicating at first, until it'd grown to be nauseating.

"I figured out who I am—sexually—with him," Jimmy admitted, eager to speak honestly, to give voice to thoughts he had contained for some time. "It made me look at myself differently."

It had been with Chris that Jimmy first had a chance to fully explore his sexuality, getting to indulge in desires that had remained hidden for years.

"It's a strange thing that happens. You know yourself theoretically, but it's not until you start actually doing things that you realize what you like and don't like. What works for you and what doesn't. It kinda redefines you. It was exciting." Jimmy's inhibitions had vanished with Chris, the sexual chemistry between them too strong to deny. The thrill of the affair fueled him with a newfound sense of confidence that he'd worn proudly, but eventually the passion had waned and great sex had no longer been enough. Spending time with Chris had become a chore as they'd struggled to find common ground in the world outside of the bedroom. Jimmy was surprised at first. Chris knew every crevice of his body. He knew what to do and how to do it, pleasing Jimmy in a way no one else had been able to. But when it came time for simple conversation, the alluring man, so skilled in the art of pleasing, was at a loss.

There was nothing to talk about, nothing to laugh about, nothing to hold them together. When they were out, Chris's attention was most often glued to his phone, and when he did engage, it was to judge someone around them—the woman passing by with the frumpy hips or the gay couple in the corner, too loud and obnoxious for his taste. Jimmy found himself entrenched in dissatisfaction, which turned to hate. Eventually he could no longer stand it.

"How did you get out of it?" Luke asked.

"With great difficulty."

Jimmy continued as the train moved from one station to the next, collecting more and more passengers with each stop. He shuddered to recall the things he had said to Chris at the end of their affair. He wasn't one to be harsh, but Chris had refused to listen. Every one of his attempts to explain his unhappiness had been deliberately ignored. Instead, Chris had used sex to quiet Jimmy and keep his troubled mind at bay. He was by no means a bad person, but Jimmy had reached his end and he fired at him without hesitation, criticizing the stupid things he said and the stupid things he liked. Jimmy attacked with the attempt to wound, unflinching and determined. Chris fired back, calling Jimmy a boring snob and criticizing his friends before storming out of the apartment. Days passed in silence before they finally met again, and by some accidental slip, they ended up in bed, their bodies longing to enjoy themselves one last time. Chris was rough and forceful, taking what he wanted without concern. Jimmy flinched in pain, but pleasure shot through him in waves and he couldn't resist. His stomach turned when they had finished. His body ached. He sprang up from Chris's bed and promised himself never to return.

Luke's mouth was slightly ajar as he stared at Jimmy. "That's intense," he whispered, peering down.

"Sorry. Too much information?"

"No," Luke replied, shaking off his discomfort with nonchalance.

Jimmy immediately regretted his decision to be candid. Perhaps some things were better left unsaid. He searched for something to say to lighten the mood but came up with nothing. Then another muffled announcement echoed through the train as it came to a screeching halt, its barely perceivable muttering filling the dead air. *"Twenty-Third Street. Next stop Fourteenth Street–Union Square."*

"Let's get off here!" Jimmy suggested as he sprang up. "Seems as good a stop as any."

Despite being Fall, it felt like spring when they exited the subway station, emerging into a landscape of greenery and unseasonable sunlight. Only the faintest chill filled the air. Luke removed his jacket and threw it over his shoulder.

"Global warming," he remarked. "It's happening."

"Yeah, but we'll be dead before the Earth burns to a crisp."

Luke's T-shirt hugged him snuggly, the slight mound of his agreeable belly kissing the thin fabric. Jimmy watched him with a smile. Chris now seemed so insignificant, a distant memory from another life that hardly amounted to much anymore. Luke was different. He had never been insignificant. Even during their time apart when Jimmy wanted nothing more than to hate him, he had remembered Luke fondly.

They gravitated, almost unknowingly, toward Gramercy Park, passing dog walkers in shorts and sweating joggers. Luke took Jimmy's hand, claiming it as his own as they strolled along the tree-lined pathway, leisurely soaking in the day.

"Our kids will suffer the consequences, though," Luke added.

"Wow, planning our future already?"

"Oh, I didn't mean—I mean individually…"

Jimmy smiled as Luke got worked up, fumbling over his words, his relaxed coolness displaced.

Jimmy squeezed his hand in assurance. "Do you want kids?"

"I do. You?"

"I can't really say for sure. When I was younger, I was certain I did, but now I don't really know. I love kids, and family is important to me, but I don't know if being a parent is for me."

"What changed from then to now?"

"Everything. I feel like I'm constantly evolving as a person. I guess I just worry that having a kid is the end of that evolution in a way. It almost has to be. You're suddenly responsible for someone else's life and upbringing. Of course your own interests take a back seat."

"But parenthood would become its own new experience to learn and grow from. If anything, I think it would only further your evolution."

Jimmy nodded agreeably. "Maybe I'm just too scared. Even just thinking about it makes me nervous. I'd be worried all the time. It'd drive me nuts."

"I think it's like anything; you get the hang of it as you go. Besides, you're good at everything. I'm sure you'd be a great parent."

Jimmy smiled as he glanced down at their hands joined together. They continued down the path in a comfortable silence, lost in their own world, the only two boys in Manhattan. When they reached the park's end, they exited through the ornate iron gates and strolled along the sidewalk. A lonely man playing the saxophone braced against the wall of the building across the street. His eyes were shut as he blew into the golden horn, gleaming beneath the sharp afternoon sun. Jimmy stopped to watch, his view obstructed by the occasional car passing on the street in front of them.

"Kenny G kinda ruined the sax, didn't he?"

Luke laughed. "What do you mean?"

"Well, maybe it's not fair to pin the blame on him alone, but I feel like you can't listen to the sax anymore and not think of bad nineties jazz."

"I guess you're right. It does sort of evoke the days of Michael Bolton and Sade."

"Hey now! Don't throw Sade in that category. Her music is timeless."

"Is it, though?" Luke asked.

"'Smooth Operator'? I still jam out to that. And she's still making great music. No one does it like Sade."

"All right, all right." Luke geared his attention to the sax player, listening intently. "Wait a minute. Is he playing a Sade song?"

"No!" Jimmy listened for a moment, doubting his own conviction. "No, right?"

"Maybe it's Kenny G. They all sound the same."

Jimmy shoved Luke, harder than expected. Luke flew back, laughing while he struggled to maintain his balance. Jimmy grabbed him and pulled him closer, taking his hand as they continued down the sidewalk. "I'm gonna play you some Sade," he said. "Show you what's up."

The city had a way of feeling most like home on the weekends, free of the urgency that made it so stifling during the week. Crowds were smaller, people more aware of their surroundings, especially a day like today when birds seemed to sing and trees dance.

"I love this neighborhood," Jimmy said as he squinted up at rays of sunlight beaming through tree branches. "It's so peaceful."

"It is kind of perfect."

"If you could live anywhere in the city, where would it be?" Jimmy asked.

"Anywhere?" Luke gazed off pensively. "Well, if I could live anywhere, then we're assuming money is not an issue?"

Jimmy nodded.

"In which case, I wouldn't choose New York at all."

"What? Really?" Jimmy asked.

"In an ideal world, I don't know that I would stay in New York," Luke admitted.

"You don't like it here?"

"I do. Of course, it's like nowhere else, but I find myself constantly craving something simpler. Everything's such a headache here. We get these tiny little moments of niceness, like today, but then most of it is kinda shit. Dealing with disgusting fucking subways and crammed bars and restaurants. We're all constantly piled on top of each other, getting angry for no reason."

Jimmy thought for a moment while his thumb drew circles on Luke's hand. "I guess I get that. It does sometimes feel like one giant struggle to survive. But—I just feel so connected to this place. I think it will always feel like home, even if I do move away."

Luke smiled. "Where would you go if you were to leave the city, and money was no issue?"

"That's a tough one. I haven't traveled enough to really know specifically where it'd be, but I agree with you; I'd want it to be some place simpler. I've always pictured myself in a small, cozy house on a hill somewhere. Lots of trees and sunlight. Lush and green. No one around for miles."

"You long for the quiet."

"I do. Sometimes. Most of the time."

"Won't you get lonely up there on the hill all by yourself?"

"Maybe there'd be space for someone else—in a guesthouse. In the back."

Luke laughed as they moved steadily away from the stillness of the park and farther into the city full of people. The sounds of traffic grew and the sidewalks filled.

"I'm kind of hungry," Luke confessed as they hurried to cross the street while the light was still in their favor.

"Oh, really?" Jimmy asked with a glare when they landed on the other side. "So the omelet wasn't sufficient?"

"Don't give me shit. You know you are too."

They entered a small, nondescript deli where a handful of patrons occupied barstools lining the perimeter.

"Hey, let's split one of those," Luke suggested, pointing to a man struggling to raise a ridiculously large sub to his mouth, bits of meat and mustard oozing out.

"That looks intense," Jimmy replied. "I'm in!"

LUKE PLOPPED THE heavy tray onto the counter near two vacant barstools. The weight of the sandwich sent the tray crashing onto the stainless-steel surface with a thud.

Jimmy approached carrying a gigantic Styrofoam cup. "All they had was 7up." He placed the ridiculously large drink down near the sub.

"7up? Score!"

"Who still drinks 7up? I honestly thought they stopped making it. Also, why'd you order a large? Look at the size of this cup!"

"If we're gonna do it," Luke replied, pointing at the enormous sub spread out across the lopsided tray, "we gotta do it right."

"So, where exactly do we begin?" Jimmy asked as he examined the sub. "This thing is like three feet long."

"I think it's best to just attack it," Luke concluded. "Grab your end."

They carefully raised the sandwich, synchronizing their every move as it inched higher, on the brink of collapsing.

"Ready?" Luke asked.

"On the count of three."

"One."

"Two."

"Three!"

They attacked the overstuffed sub from both ends. The center of the ominous bridge of meat sagged as lumps of mustard and mayo spewed out. Jimmy placed his hand under the center, supporting the weight while struggling to chew. Luke worked to hold back a laugh, his mouth filled beyond capacity. They stared at each other as they fought to swallow. Jimmy signaled, and they gracefully lowered the sub back to the plate.

"I can't even tell if it's any good," Jimmy finally managed to utter. "Pass me the 7up."

Luke took a gulp first and then slid the gigantic cup across the counter. "It's delicious," he mumbled.

Jimmy took a swig of 7up and swallowed hard as he squinted in pain. "I think I've actually had enough."

"One bite! Come on."

"Your eyes are watering."

"Are they? It was worth it."

"How are we going to finish the rest of it?" Jimmy asked.

Luke reached over and, with a swift tug, yanked the sub into two pieces. He smiled gleefully as he picked up his half, displaying it to Jimmy.

"Why didn't we do that in the first place?" Jimmy asked.

"Wouldn't have been nearly as fun."

Jimmy was careful to take a smaller, more manageable bite, but the sub was falling apart at every seam, the mess almost too much to handle.

"Well, next time you're in the mood for a three-foot sub, you know where to come," Luke said with a wink as he chewed.

"It's a good thing we stumbled on this place. Can't wait to tell everyone I know."

"Somehow, I think your friends wouldn't exactly love this place?"

"Why not?" Jimmy asked.

"I imagine their taste is somewhat more elevated."

"You obviously haven't met my friends. I wouldn't exactly call them elevated."

"Well, when can I meet them?"

Jimmy smiled at Luke, whose lips were lined with mustard as he peered up from behind the sandwich, his cheeks filled like a chipmunk.

"One of these days," Jimmy replied, holding back a laugh.

Chapter Seven

THE BAR WAS nearly filled to capacity, an eclectic mix of gay, straight, and otherwise. Neon-pink lights lined the walls; confetti covered the floor. A drag show had just finished, and the group of extravagantly dressed performers gathered near the makeshift stage, barking at each other, attempting to settle a dispute. Jimmy stood with Blake along the perimeter of the small dance floor, getting pushed and shoved occasionally as people made their way in and out of the cramped arena. Charlie approached with a drink for himself and Jimmy. Jimmy downed half of it.

"Thirsty much?" Charlie asked as he stared.

Jimmy nodded anxiously, already working on the remainder of the cocktail.

"What the fuck! Where's mine?" Blake shouted.

Charlie laughed at Blake, and then geared his attention to the drag queens. "What's happening over there?"

"Shit's about to go down," Jimmy replied.

One of the performers removed her heels, preparing for attack. Blake sighed, loud enough to be heard over the commotion.

"Why didn't you get Blake a drink?" Jimmy asked Charlie.

"*She* didn't ask for one."

Blake rolled his eyes. "You're an asshole."

Jimmy had little energy to mitigate whatever feud was brewing between his friends. His mind was elsewhere as he scoured the crowd, anxiously waiting for Luke, dreading his arrival, but also longing for Luke to emerge and save him from a night of useless arguing. He was now twenty minutes late. Panic settled in as Jimmy wondered if he had changed his mind, if all the doubt that once stood in Luke's way had reemerged, reminding him of why it hadn't worked out the first time around. Maybe it was better this way, Jimmy told himself. Better it ended now before the roots were too firmly in place.

"You know what your problem is?" Charlie shouted to Blake. "Your mouth has no filter."

Blake laughed. "You're one to talk!"

"What is going on here?" Jimmy barked, flustered by an overwhelming mix of confused emotions.

"Ask *her*!" Charlie shouted, pointing to Blake.

"Who knows? It could be anything," Blake replied calmly.

Charlie gasped, stunned into silence for a moment, before complaining to Jimmy about how rude Blake had been when meeting his boyfriend. "Not to mention, we've been dating for months, and he only now finds the time to answer my calls."

"What?" Blake interjected coolly. "He's hot and stupid. There's nothing wrong with that. It's not an insult, just an observation."

Jimmy glared at Blake.

Charlie shook his head in disbelief, his resolve to fight back diminishing. "It's not even worth it. You're never going to see yourself."

"What's that supposed to mean?" Blake asked.

"You think you're better than everyone else," Charlie replied, notably calmer. "But the truth is you're so fucking miserable, you can't stand to see anyone else happy. You want all of us to be just as miserable as you. Well, guess what? You're shit out of luck. Jimmy's all boyfriend-ed up too. So it's just you, sweetie. All alone and miserable."

"Well—" Jimmy interjected. "I don't know if I'd call us boyfriends."

"Okay, Charlie," Blake replied. "If that's how you want to see it, that's fine. Different perspectives is all." He shifted his attention to Jimmy. "So—where is this mysterious lover boy?"

Jimmy gulped. "He must be on his way. I'm sure he'll be here soon."

Blake had a way of finding the negative in any given situation, his outlook most often bleak, but he meant well. He masked a certain sadness behind a frank indifference to most things, but Jimmy trusted his opinion, valued it even, especially considering the familiar haze in which he now found himself so deeply trapped. In some strange, sadistic way, Jimmy longed for Blake to strike it down, to deem Luke unworthy. Perhaps, it might snap him out of his current dreamscape and prevent any further heartache.

"So excited to meet him," Charlie said, feigning a smile for Jimmy, though it was obvious his feelings were still hurt and reconciliation with Blake was nowhere in sight. It was just about the worst time for Luke to meet Jimmy's friends, but luckily, he had not yet arrived. There was still hope he had bailed and Jimmy might save himself the embarrassment.

"This is the same guy who ghosted you, right?" Blake asked.

"Well," Jimmy began, now regretting the less than favorable image he had created of Luke, "I think maybe it's different now."

"It's totally different," Charlie replied. "Don't listen to ass-face. He can't help how bitter he is."

"Does it feel different?" Blake asked, ignoring Charlie.

"In certain ways."

"Does *he* feel different?" Charlie questioned, offering his own morsel of doubt to the mix of confused emotions.

"He does," Jimmy replied. "He's more certain, intense even. Honestly, I think that's what scares me a little. Why is he suddenly so certain when he wasn't before?"

Blake and Charlie grew silent, troubled looks displayed unabashedly on unnerved faces.

A surge of panic filled Jimmy as his own words echoed through his ears. "But look, this is not even worth discussing. It's nothing. We are just hanging out. It's not like we're a couple or anything. I don't even know if he'll show up tonight."

"He better show up," Blake interjected.

Jimmy forced a smile and returned to his drink, growing more certain of his failure. Maybe he was being ghosted all over again. Luke was not one to be late. Maybe he had changed his mind. Even so, Jimmy knew there was no one to blame but himself for falling into the same trap. Charlie and Blake now stood where his plate of cheese and crackers once had, bearing witness to his embarrassment. Their concern was alarming. They too had the same reservations, only validating Jimmy's. He peered around the dense crowd, blaring pop remixes and loud conversations filling the packed space, searching for a hole to hide his head in. He contemplated leaving, slipping off to the bathroom only to run home. He could likely make an easy enough escape. His attention continued to wander until finally landing on Luke.

Luke, looking more dapper than usual, stood frozen in a sea of dancing strangers who swayed and glided past him in droves. A troubled look masked his usual self-assurance as he scoured the crowd, noticeably uncomfortable and out of place. His hands were pressed in his pockets, sweat beaded from his forehead. Jimmy's fears dissipated as his focus rested on Luke. He had never seen him look so worried. Jimmy longed to rush in and save him from whatever discomfort he was feeling, to whisk him away from this bewildering, overcrowded place. Luke's expression grew bright when his gaze finally met Jimmy's. His calm disposition returned as he drew closer, parting the sea of strangers with ease, his attention all the while fixed on Jimmy as he approached.

"There you are." Luke's quiet whisper was barely audible when he arrived. He wrapped his arm around Jimmy's waist, touched Jimmy's cheek with his lips as he leaned in. "It's nuts in here."

"Well, who do we have here?" Charlie asked, wide-eyed.

Jimmy made the necessary introductions, his head lost again to that glowing haze of intoxication. Luke stood close by his side. Jimmy longed to grab him, to claim him as his own, to laugh in his friends' faces and that of his own pesky doubt. But he was quick to silence his urge. They had not been proven wrong yet, not entirely. Only time would tell and he was in no immediate rush to find out.

"It's good to meet you guys," Luke said confidently, his magnetic charm restored. "I've heard a lot about you."

"Only good things, I hope," Charlie replied with a smirk.

"Only the best."

"So, Luke," Blake interjected. "Tell us again, how did you guys meet?"

Jimmy glared at Blake's lack of restraint, his breath suspended as he turned to Luke.

"Well, we met through mutual friends," Luke began, seemingly aware he was on display. "A while ago actually. But we haven't seen each other in a few years."

"A few years?" Blake questioned. "Wow. And how did you guys lose touch for so long?"

Luke smiled politely in response to the ongoing interrogation.

"We ran into each other at the art center a few weeks ago," Jimmy replied sharply. "You know that."

"Oh right, right," Blake submitted. "The art center."

"Have you been here before, Luke?" Charlie asked.

"No, can't say that I have. I sadly don't frequent Brooklyn as much as I probably should. It's a cool bar, though. Strange, but cool."

"Where do you live?" Blake asked.

Luke swallowed hard as if already aware his response might ignite further disdain. "I'm in Midtown."

"Oh. Midtown," Blake replied coldly. "Whereabouts?"

"Forty-First, between Ninth and Eighth."

Charlie winced in disgust. "Near Times Square?"

"God. Who would want to live there?" Blake exclaimed. "Doesn't it get frustrating?"

"It can. But where I am is a bit removed from the main tourist hub, so I don't really feel it."

"And you like it there?" Charlie asked. Jimmy's body twitched with discomfort. He longed to lash out at his friends, to force them to behave, but any such move would only worsen the situation.

"It's probably not the best neighborhood, but I do like that it's so central. I'm only a few blocks from where I'm working right now, so it's nice to be able to walk and not have to ride the train every day."

Blake gasped. "Even I would put up with Midtown if I could walk to work. You could go home for lunch."

"Afternoon naps!" Charlie exclaimed.

"Oh man, they're the best!" Luke replied. "Except for when I crash too hard and sleep in."

"You go home in the middle of the day?" Jimmy asked.

"Sometimes," Luke answered with a grin intended for Jimmy's eyes only. "But only when there's not much going on."

Jimmy was relieved to see Luke smiling again. The tension had lifted. To his surprise, Luke grew more enthusiastic, more boisterous as the night progressed, earnestly engaging in conversation with Blake and Charlie. Jimmy admired his confidence. Others seemed to as well. It commanded respect. Luke had a way of seeming at home and staying true to himself regardless of his company. Jimmy observed the comfortable union of his two very different worlds as his friends laughed and argued and carried on. At times, Luke treaded lightly across sometimes unfamiliar terrain, restraining his retorts, preventing any sort of hostile disagreement from brewing, but he never backed down fully. Jimmy took pleasure in seeing Blake surrender from time to time, even agreeing, on occasion, with the gallant new addition to the group.

What was, however, most endearing was Luke's effort. It was not for the sake of making new friends that he had ventured out to Brooklyn, shouting to be heard in a crowded bar that was far from his scene. Perhaps, Jimmy began to think, it might be safe to surrender to what he was feeling, to give in to the desire to be with Luke without reservation.

"You need a drink." Jimmy took Luke's hand, desperate for a moment alone. "We'll be back," he said to Charlie and Blake. "You guys want anything?"

A space cleared at the bar as they approached. Luke grabbed a vacant barstool and plopped down on it, spinning around to rest his back against the counter.

Jimmy landed between his open legs. "Are you having an okay time?"

"I'm having a great time. Charlie and Blake are a lot of fun. I wasn't sure at first, but I think we warmed up to each other pretty quickly."

"I can see that."

"Sorry I was late," apologized Luke.

"Where were you?"

"Did you think I wasn't going to show?"

"Honestly," Jimmy replied, "I didn't really care either way."

"Oh, really? Well, I could leave if you'd prefer."

"Nah. You're already here. Might as well stay."

Luke tucked his fingers into Jimmy's pockets and yanked him closer. "I wanted to make you sweat a little, so I thought I'd take my time."

"Don't give yourself too much credit. There was no sweating." Jimmy stepped back, resisting the strong urge to submit to Luke's command. "You look nice," he added.

"Do I?" Luke asked appreciatively.

His navy-blue sweater wrapped around his torso snuggly, the taut fabric making his physique appear firmer than it actually was. His shoulders seemed broader, his chest more pronounced. Jimmy longed to wrap his arms around the snug, knitted material but was too busy playing it cool to entertain such thoughts for long.

"You also look very warm," Jimmy noted as he wiped sweat from Luke's forehead.

"I know. It's hot as balls in here," he replied, pushing his sleeves up to his elbows. "But it's cold outside. How exactly are you supposed to accommodate for this sort of thing?"

Luke's slender forearms glistened, a few pronounced veins standing temptingly on hairless skin. Jimmy caressed Luke's soft, tender skin, wet with sweat.

"Quite the conundrum you find yourself in," Jimmy uttered, his attention fixed on Luke's glistening arms.

"Quite," Luke responded, his voice now smaller. "You, however, seem to be more appropriately prepared." Luke reached his legs out and wrapped them around Jimmy's, skillfully using them to draw Jimmy closer. "You clearly have more practice at this sort of thing than I do."

"What? Getting dressed?"

"Gay bars."

"I hate to burst your bubble, buddy, but this isn't a gay bar. It's just Brooklyn."

"The half-naked go-go boy over there might disagree."

"I don't think he works here," Jimmy replied, attention fixed on Luke. "He's up there on his own accord." Jimmy's nose touched Luke's as he leaned close, but he resisted the urge to pounce. "Do you want to go?"

"Already?" Luke questioned. "I just got here."

"It's been over an hour."

"Wouldn't it look bad? I don't want your friends to think I stole you away."

Jimmy smiled as he stepped back. "Okay, we'll stay. What do you want to drink?"

He pried himself away, gained the bartender's attention, and placed his order. The beers came pounding down with a thud as another vacant stool presented itself. Jimmy claimed it and shuffled closer to Luke who followed suit, metal stools screeching against concrete floors. Their legs interlocked until they finally had no room to move farther. Luke took Jimmy's thigh into his possession and bounced it back and forth between his hands like an amused cat playing with a ball of yarn.

"I did worry for a minute that you weren't going to show," Jimmy admitted as he sipped his beer, already feeling drunk.

"Really?" Luke grinned. "My plan worked."

Jimmy reached down and pinched at the bit of flesh beneath Luke's knee. Luke winced in pain.

"I'm kidding!" he exclaimed. "I hadn't planned on being late." He paused for a moment, as if deciding whether to continue with the truth. "Honestly, I was a bit anxious. I changed three times before I settled on this stupid sweater, which, needless to say, I now regret."

Jimmy laughed as he imagined Luke trying on outfits while he waited at the bar, doubt-stricken and preparing for the worst. "You changed three times?" he asked, smiling.

"I didn't know what to wear. Honestly, I considered asking you, but I thought that would look stupid." Luke's face grew a shade redder.

"Why were you so worried about what to wear?"

"I just wanted to make a good impression. I didn't really know what to expect with your friends, and they're important to you. This whole thing isn't really my scene. I didn't want to look overdressed, or underdressed. It was tricky."

"Well, my friend, you're the most dapper man in here. And I have to admit that sweater is really doing it for me. So, job well done."

"Oh, really? Good to know."

Their gazes remained locked. Luke's smile gradually fell, and a heavy silence grew, the rightness between them dangerously evident. Its weight filled the space, too obvious to ignore. Luke opened his mouth as if to speak, but seemed to be at a loss for words.

Jimmy looked away, the building pressure forcing him to retreat. He turned his attention to Luke's knee, stationed between his legs, and rested his hand there as he swayed gently to a familiar song. Luke reached for his drink, took a giant gulp, and then another.

"I saw them live a little while ago," Jimmy noted, pointing to the speakers overhead. "They were great."

"Who is it?" Luke asked, trying to listen to the lyrics of the song amidst the crowd's clamor. "I don't think I've ever heard it."

"Friendly Fires. Never heard of them?"

"No," Luke replied. "But my taste in music can't really be trusted. Not a fan of Sade, remember?"

"Of course! You know nothing." Jimmy's body swayed more boldly as the song grew fuller. "Hey, let's dance," he suggested as he reached for his beer.

"No," Luke responded, quickly finishing his drink.

"Come on. It'll be fun."

"I really—I don't dance." Luke grew flustered.

"I can't dance either. I just bob up and down effectively enough. I do find that if you add a little side sway," Jimmy said, slithering his body from left to right like a snake gaining traction, "the overall look is a little more convincing."

Luke laughed heartily as he watched Jimmy make a fool of himself. "Okay," he replied, giving in. "With that by my side, no one will be watching me anyway."

Jimmy rose and grabbed Luke's hand, escorting him through the crowd to the tiny dance floor. It was only a few feet wide, a sort of makeshift area barely large enough to accommodate the mass of people. The crowd was fitting for the venue, groups of eccentrically dressed drunk people convulsing in a compact arena of sweat and euphoria. Luke stayed close to Jimmy, hopping on one leg with an uncomfortable grimace plastered on his face. Jimmy grabbed his hips and, taking them into his command, swayed them from left to right. Luke raised his hands in the air, laughing as he added his own flare to the movement. His expression grew brighter and his inhibitions seemed to vanish as he looked around, noticeably invigorated by the crowd, strangers dancing wildly. Jimmy stepped back and watched adoringly. Luke's lanky arms soared through the air, and his long, pronounced neck bobbed like a rooster searching for worms, a crooked smile stretched across his face. His delight was infectious.

The music blurred, along with the crowd's shouts and cheers, merging into silence as everything but Luke grew hazy. A sudden urge to claim him filled Jimmy. He longed to hold him near, to feel Luke's body pressed against his own. He ached to know everything about him, every trivial detail of Luke's life—to know what he had been like as a kid, to know what his parents looked like and sounded like, to know and understand what had shaped who he was.

Luke's eyes shut as the music enveloped him. He moved more and more freely, like someone who had never danced before as the song changed from one song to another. He panted for air, out of breath, pushed at his sleeves as they fell. Jimmy approached and offered his assistance, helping to free him of the burden. Luke grabbed Jimmy's arm and held him close as the pulse of their bodies harmonized, Luke's chaotic rhythm mellowing to match Jimmy's gentler glide.

Sweat dripped from Luke's forehead, passing his lush brows all the way down to his lips. Jimmy wiped him clean again. Luke grinned and pressed his face close, rubbing his cheek against Jimmy's, his dampness softening its glide. He opened his mouth, and warm breath charged forward. Jimmy's body tingled. He felt the sharp graze of Luke's teeth across his cheek, the moistness of his lips against bare skin. Jimmy pulled Luke closer so that every part of his body might feel his closeness. Their lips slid across each other's faces until finally crashing together. Luke's hand rested on Jimmy's lower back. His grip grew firm and commanding. Jimmy found his way into Luke's tight, heavy sweater, sliding his hand across Luke's sweaty stomach like skates on ice, working his way to Luke's back where a hot trail of wetness ran down his spine. Jimmy grabbed at flesh as he pulled him even closer. Luke winced in pleasure as the brawl between their tongues grew more and more frantic.

"Let's get out of here," Luke moaned, no longer able to contain his growing excitement.

Jimmy agreed with a nod as he continued pecking at Luke's lips. "It's probably easier," he mumbled between kisses, "to get to your place from here."

"You think?" Luke struggled to ask.

"Do you not want me over?" Jimmy asked as he peeled away slightly.

Luke drew Jimmy close again and pressed his forehead against Jimmy's, resting it there with his mouth ajar as he caught his breath. Their bodies still swayed ever so slightly, lost in their own world amidst a sea of unaware strangers. "I just worry we won't be comfortable there. It's a tiny shithole."

"You have a bed?" Jimmy asked as he peered into the large, dark eyes so close to his own he could barely focus on them.

"Yes. I have a bed."

"And no roommates?"

"You know I live alone."

"Well then, we'll make do."

Charlie and Blake hadn't entered Jimmy's mind until he was well on his way with Luke, nestled comfortably in the back seat of a stranger's car. He hadn't thought to find them before he left. His body urged him in another direction, the familiar haze that seemed to follow Luke blurring his vision of anything in the periphery. No one else seemed to matter but Luke, whose head rested heavy on his shoulder. Jimmy's head grew tired too, and it fell onto Luke's as his eyes shut.

"We're here," said the jovial driver as he stopped the car.

Luke quickly sprang to action, revived and fully coherent as he exited the car and ushered Jimmy toward his building. They took a short elevator ride up to the third floor. Jimmy was relieved to be free of the decrepit lift. It rattled and shook, its precariously frail metal doors quivering as it made its way up. Once out of its confines, they entered a narrow hall. A harsh fluorescent glow flickered across its bare gray walls casting a chilling air over the whole scene. It felt like an asylum of sorts, or at least what Jimmy imagined one looked like. He anchored himself to Luke's arm as they continued down the long, treacherous corridor, worried that its previous inhabitants still lurked in its walls and beneath its floors. Luke rested his hand on Jimmy's, comforting him as though he too knew of the spirits that roamed the passageway. Finally, they reached the hall's end and came to a heavy, steel door, sealed with not one but three separate locks. Luke worked from his ring of keys to open it as Jimmy anxiously waited, looking forward to the safety of Luke's home on the other side. They would, no doubt, be free of the evil hallway soon enough. To his dismay, the robust door opened to an even more eerie set of stairs.

"Are you serious?" Jimmy exclaimed, no longer able to hold back his frail nerves.

"Hey, I warned you. Don't worry. It's just one level up."

The service stairs seemed more like a last resort than a daily connection. Its rails were thin, more decorative than utilitarian, providing little security from the three-story fall that lay waiting below. Jimmy shuddered to use them, relying on the arm of his escort as his sole protection.

"I thought my walk-up was bad. You do this every day?"

"You get used to it."

They made the ascent to the top of the stairwell where they were greeted by a lonely but pleasant door—far less ominous than the last they had entered. It was sealed more reasonably by one shiny, steel lock. It glimmered with newness against the surface of the wooden door, freshly painted with a thick coat of white. A sticker was planted at its center, the number five etched in gold.

"Where's one through four?" Jimmy asked.

"I don't know, actually. I always wondered that."

Jimmy laughed, eager to find some humor in the bleak landscape. "You don't know if you have neighbors or not?"

"I think I'm the only one," Luke replied as he turned the key. "I think they just randomly picked the number five."

"Maybe it was the only sticker they had left."

"I wouldn't be surprised. I think it's actually more of a service closet that they advertised as an apartment."

Luke opened the door to darkness, but anything seemed better than the evil stairs and gloomy corridor that they had just traversed. Jimmy shut the door behind him as Luke walked ahead to the other end of the tiny studio apartment and switched on a floor lamp. Anywhere else, the miniscule light fixture would have provided only dim ambiance, but it more than adequately filled the miniature space. The wall opposite the door was bare except for a small shelf that housed only a handful of books and DVDs. To the right was another bare wall with a window only about two feet high and scarcely one foot wide. It overlooked a brick building merely inches away from its glass. The pane was held open by a stack of books resting strategically on the ledge.

"Why is your window open?" Jimmy asked.

"I can't control the heat, so if I don't open the window it turns into a sauna in here."

"Oh. Makes sense." Jimmy feigned a smile, though he worried about the state of the unregulated heater so near to the tiny bed.

A plush brown couch, decrepit but inviting, sat squarely in the center of the room, facing a small TV held up by a charming wooden stand, the sort of flea market find Jimmy delighted in. To its right was a small stove, sink, and refrigerator, which appeared to make up the dwelling's kitchen. Everything was fairly neat and orderly, except for the few articles of clothing that seemed to have no designated housing, gaming remotes scattered around the TV, and dishes piled high near the stove. Luke scrambled to pick up a pair of sneakers and socks that lay at the foot of the bed.

"It's cute in here," Jimmy said as he finished surveying the small space.

"It's a dump. I know."

"Not at all. It seems very comfortable. Honestly, I'm just glad to be on firm ground." Jimmy sank into the sofa with ease, its plush cushions surrounding him.

Luke approached and joined him on the couch, unexpectedly careful not to get too close. "Thanks for inviting me out tonight."

"Thanks for coming," Jimmy replied.

"I had a lot of fun actually."

"I saw that."

"I know I made a fool of myself with my pathetic attempt at dancing."

"Are you kidding?" Jimmy replied. "You've got moves, my friend."

Luke laughed as he threw himself more comfortably against the plush sofa.

"I had fun just watching you have fun," Jimmy added.

Luke kicked off his shoes and turned to Jimmy with a grin, his pearly-white teeth beaming. His hair was disheveled, his hue still rosy. This was Luke at home. Jimmy approached, eager to taste him. He reached down to the end of Luke's sweater and pried it off. Luke assisted, lifting off the back of the couch and raising his arms as the heavy fabric peeled off his wet skin. He sighed as if relieved to finally be free of the burden. Jimmy stopped for a moment to admire Luke's bareness. His smooth, hairless skin glistened beneath the lamp's faint light. Jimmy glided his hand across Luke's soft stomach and flat, adorably undefined chest as he took in every detail, observing every region of Luke's bare torso. When he had satisfied his curiosity, Jimmy mounted him.

Luke unbuttoned Jimmy's shirt, working his way to the final button at the collar with precision. He reached for flesh, throwing the shirt to the floor. He followed the light trail of hair that started at Jimmy's collarbone with his fingers, working his way down Jimmy's chest, swirling around his nipples. He leaned in to taste Jimmy's nipple. His tongue circled around the tender flesh. His arms wrapped tightly around Jimmy and carefully guided him to lie down on the other end of the couch. He unbuttoned Jimmy's jeans and pulled them down before slipping out of his own.

Luke was cautious when he first entered Jimmy, gauging Jimmy's comfort level before proceeding further. He held Jimmy close, his arms under Jimmy's shoulders as he thrust in and out. Jimmy wrapped his legs around Luke's torso, his eyes rolling back in satisfaction. Their bodies joined together as sweat mixed. Jimmy bit on Luke's ear, breathing heavily as his body filled with warmth. He grabbed locks of Luke's shaggy hair as he cried out, teetering back and forth between pain and pleasure as Luke's resolve deepened, the force of his thrusts strengthening. Jimmy's eyes opened to Luke's face glistening with sweat, mouth ajar as he panted. He kissed his moist lips, still tugging at his hair as he inhaled his scent. They sank deeper and deeper into the plush cushions of the couch. It creaked, struggling to bear the load. Luke bent and twisted, Jimmy pulled and tugged, their bodies churning, the world around them silent.

Chapter Eight

THE TINY APARTMENT felt more familiar in the morning, though it was hard to tell if it even was morning. The brick wall facing the small window prevented much light from entering. Luke's head lay on Jimmy's shoulder. His hand rested on Jimmy's chest, rising and falling as Jimmy breathed in and out.

"Are you hungry?" Luke mumbled.

"Not really." Jimmy yawned as he stretched his body across the bed, lifting Luke along with him.

Luke pried himself off Jimmy and rolled onto his back.

"What time is it?" Jimmy asked. Judging from the sliver of cool light that made its way into the apartment, it was likely still early.

Luke replied with a shrug.

Jimmy turned to rest his head on Luke's chest. "You're sweaty."

"I sweat easily."

"I can tell," Jimmy replied while gliding his cheek along Luke's moist skin. Luke draped his arm around Jimmy and squeezed tightly until it hurt. Jimmy was amused for a moment but demanded he stop.

"Last night was fun," Luke noted suggestively as he loosened his grip.

It was likely the best, Jimmy thought, but he knew better than to admit it. With others, there had always been a need to adjust to better fit into the role designated for him. With Luke, he was himself. They fit together with ease.

"Long overdue," Jimmy declared.

Luke chuckled, squeezing Jimmy's arm. "Well, was it worth the wait?"

"Eh, I've had better," Jimmy replied as he rubbed Luke's chest.

Luke scoffed. "How old were you the first time you had sex?"

"Define sex."

"Well—first sexual experience."

Jimmy thought about it. The moment itself was clear as day, but it took some time to remember his age.

"Fourteen, I think."

"That's young," Luke replied. "Who with?"

Jimmy grew embarrassed. "Sal. He was sort of my cousin."

"What!" Luke exclaimed. "You fucked your cousin?"

"No, wait! It sounds more scandalous than it really is. He isn't actually my cousin, but we grew up like cousins. His mom was my mom's best friend growing up. They spent all their time together. She was basically my aunt."

"And Sal was basically your cousin."

"Basically."

Luke insisted on hearing the details. Jimmy continued, confessing secrets he had forever kept to himself. He found some thrill in retelling the tale. It seemed funny now, two boys exploring themselves.

"It was barely even sexual. More scientific."

Luke laughed. "I wouldn't exactly call having his dick in your mouth scientific."

"All right, all right. What about you?" Jimmy asked. "Was it love at first sight with your next-door neighbor?"

"Not exactly." Luke hesitated. "It was an online hookup, actually."

"Really? How old were you?" Jimmy asked.

"I was older, maybe seventeen."

"Was Grindr even a thing then?"

"I'm sure it was, but I didn't know about it. I found this guy in a chat room of all places. Remember those?"

Jimmy raised his head, quickly intrigued. He rested his chin on Luke's chest so as to get a better view while Luke retold the story.

"I was confused," Luke admitted. "And I was getting older. I needed to figure shit out."

Luke and the mysterious internet figure chatted for some time before meeting. They had common interests and were both just as inexperienced. It had made him feel safe, Luke admitted, to be talking to someone in the same situation. They discussed TV and movies and video games for weeks before building up the courage to meet. When they finally did, Luke was pleasantly surprised to discover the guy was not far from what he had imagined. They met at a park, central enough to both their homes. Luke was eager to engage, viewing the night as his first real date. But the guy had other plans.

"It just got out of my control. We were sitting on a bench just talking, and suddenly he started kissing my neck and out of nowhere starts rubbing my dick."

Jimmy stared, wide-eyed and amused, eager to hear more.

"Next thing I know," Luke continued, "he's on his knees, unzipping my pants. Trust me, it's not at all what I had it mind, but once he started, I couldn't stop him."

"So you let him suck you off? Right there in public?"

"Yeah. I just kinda let it happen."

Jimmy laughed. "He just couldn't resist!"

"What can I say? Boys just fall to their knees."

"What happened after?" Jimmy asked.

"Nothing. I was confused and disoriented. It felt good, obviously, but it's not at all what I was expecting. It was stupid of me, but I kinda thought we were dating. We talked to each other every night for weeks. I thought, maybe, it was the beginning of something."

Jimmy imagined a young and disappointed Luke returning home, alone and confused. His shattered night was not a far cry from Jimmy's own moments of disillusionment.

"Did you ever speak to him again?" Jimmy asked.

"No. We went our separate ways and that was it."

Jimmy returned his cheek to its resting place on Luke's chest. He wrapped his leg around Luke's, nestling closer. "So who gives better head? Internet boy or me?"

Luke chuckled. "How would I know? Unless you blew me while I was sleeping, you have yet to go there."

Jimmy sprang up on all fours, surprised by the oversight. "We're settling this right now. Take off your boxers," he commanded as he crawled down the bed.

Luke followed Jimmy's orders, laughing deviously as he ripped his boxers off and swung his hands behind his head, relaxed and ready. "Have at it!"

Chapter Nine

"I'M NOT SAYING I don't agree with you," Luke persisted. "Of course it's better to buy organic. I'm just saying it's not so simple for most people. Organic is expensive." Luke grabbed a handful of cashews from the nearby bin and raised his full palm to Jimmy as if the mere sight of the nut was proof enough of his point.

"You can't just grab it like that!" Jimmy barked. "That's why there's a scooper." Jimmy opened his small plastic bag, already filled with almonds and cranberries, and forced Luke to pour the cashews into the mix. "Now you've contaminated the whole bunch, you farmer's-market-hating tyrant."

"I don't hate farmer's markets. Local farmers!" Luke shouted, fists raised in support.

They continued down the small, nearly empty row of vendors. Only a few other customers roamed the quiet market. The selection was understandably sparse given the cold, harsh air, mixed nuts and cakes taking the place of the usual array of fresh produce. Jimmy was determined, nonetheless, to find the best ingredients available to make dinner.

"So you'd rather we just give our money to giant corporations who are injecting our food with god-knows-what so we can save two quarters," Jimmy rebutted.

"You act like you're going to get cancer if you eat tomatoes from Key Food."

"Key Food!" Jimmy exclaimed. "Are you serious? I'd get way worse than just cancer. The workers there probably piss on the produce to keep it fresh."

Luke sighed, getting more agitated. "You're such a snot," he said under his breath, but loud enough to be heard.

"I don't think avoiding Key Food makes me a snot," Jimmy replied. "Just smart."

Jimmy enjoyed getting Luke worked up. It seemed easier these days. His speech became hasty. His mouth seemed to dry, prompting the need for his tongue to spring into action and sporadically wet his pink lips. The sharpness of his petite nose grew more severe. There was something undeniably attractive about Luke's angry face. When he argued a point, his hands took flight, more deliberate in their motion than usual, conducting the orchestra with a stern force. Jimmy admired the sincerity of Luke's conviction, even when it countered his own opinion.

"At the very least you're an elitist," Luke added.

"Elitist—all right, I'll take it. I do know I'm better than everyone else, so I guess it makes sense."

Winter was in full swing. Jimmy's feather-filled coat was zipped up to his chin. Its soft padding surrounded his body almost entirely. Luke tugged at the billowing coat from behind, unwelcomingly tampering with Jimmy's robust suit of armor.

"In your giant coat, you look like a penguin waddling around on the hunt for overpriced organic vegetables."

"I'm not trying to be cute," Jimmy asserted. "It's fucking freezing."

"Yeah, I know. Wouldn't it be nice to be in a grocery store with central heat right about now?" Luke wrapped his arms around him, cuddling Jimmy like a giant stuffed animal. "I like you as a giant penguin."

Jimmy laughed as his palm fell on Luke's cold, dry hands. "You're freezing."

"I'm not as prepared as you are."

"You never are."

Jimmy and Luke had grown inseparable during the past two months. The rhythm of their daily lives fit together with ease. But certain moments stood out, times when his mind sprang up in attention and he became aware of the significance of what was happening. Before Luke, Jimmy hadn't known what it was like to shop for groceries with another, to prepare a meal for an intimate someone. There were, in fact, so many little thrills he had already grown accustomed to enjoying—thrills he'd only ever imagined that somehow had become commonplace. He could now guarantee that he would not be sleeping alone on a Friday or Saturday night. His otherwise quiet apartment would be filled with chatter and laughter and sex. The sleepovers even spread from just Friday and Saturday nights, to the occasional weeknight. On such occasions, Luke would arrive sporting his ragged duffel bag, his work clothes carelessly tossed in the unnecessarily large accessory.

Jimmy admired watching Luke get ready for work in the morning, the dark circles under his eyes still heavy from the weight of sleep. Luke's speed was impressive. Fifteen minutes was all he needed to slip on his snug khakis, button his shirt, and slick back his hair. Jimmy, on the other hand, was lucky if an hour was enough. He had made a habit of taking his time with breakfast, enjoying an unrushed shower, leisurely getting dressed. Luke still woke with Jimmy on mornings spent together, staying in bed for a while longer, deliberately creeping through his usual routine, allowing their schedules to coincide more closely so they could ride the train together.

"Wait a minute," Jimmy commanded as he dug through the many pockets in his cumbersome coat. Finally, he pulled out a set of black, knitted gloves and handed them to Luke.

"You have extra gloves?" Luke asked while thrusting them on his cold, brittle hands.

"They're my backup pair."

"Backup pair?"

"Yeah," Jimmy said, the concept completely rational in his eyes. "You never know when you'll need another pair of gloves."

"But you're wearing gloves already."

"I know, but I'm always worried I'll leave them somewhere and be gloveless."

"Somehow I don't imagine you losing your gloves," Luke replied.

"I don't think I ever have, actually. But I left them at a restaurant once and had to run back to get them, so it is a possibility."

Luke smiled as he rubbed his gloved palms together, warm and protected. "Well, I'm appreciating your preparedness right about now, however strange it may be. What else you got in that thing? Ooh, do you have a backup scarf?"

"No." Jimmy glared. "But good idea," he whispered under his breath, continuing down the path. His search for the perfect eggplant had become the search for any available eggplant.

"This just proves my point."

"How's that?" Jimmy asked, only partially paying attention as he shopped.

"You're exactly the kind of person who buys organic."

"And what kind of person is that?"

"The kind that can afford to have two sets of gloves with him at any given time. Of course you have the luxury of worrying about where your vegetables come from, but the average working-class family doesn't have the time, energy, or resources to really give a shit. So they eat whatever. We can't blame them for eating badly. It's just out of necessity."

"I never blamed anyone. Besides, that's why there are co-ops," Jimmy replied. "You don't even have to pay for your food."

"Do you really think anyone who is struggling to pay their rent by working two jobs has time to volunteer at a hippie-run co-op in Brooklyn so that they can buy organic tomatoes?"

Luke's tone sharpened. He sounded outraged, but Jimmy remained focused on his own plight as he scoured the sparse selection of vegetables available, devising new plans for his meal that would better utilize the options at his disposal. He placed his hand on a particularly appealing bundle of brussels sprouts.

"Do you like brussels sprouts?" Jimmy asked, raising them toward Luke.

"What?" Luke looked at the strange vegetable disinterestedly. "I guess. I don't know that I've ever had them, actually."

"You've never had brussels sprouts?"

"Are you even listening to me?"

"Yes, of course I am," Jimmy replied as he paid for his new find. "Co-ops, poor people, tomatoes. I heard you."

Luke rolled his eyes. "Yeah, that about sums it up."

"I don't appreciate you insinuating that I am somehow better off than most people. I bought those gloves from some guy selling weird key chains and hats on the side of the street for like, two dollars."

"Oh, please," Luke barked, revving up again. "Of course you're better off than most people. We both are."

"Speak for yourself. I ride the bus just like everyone else in this city."

"Only when your usual train's not running! You live alone in a one-bedroom in New York City. You buy fancy nuts at the organic market and carry around extra gloves on the off chance you might lose your original pair. I'd say you're better off."

"I live in Queens," Jimmy responded as he sifted through the items in his bag, mentally arranging the ingredients as Luke caught his breath and gathered his composure. Jimmy was, for the most part, pleased with his findings. It fell tragically short of his original plan, but he was confident it would suffice. Besides, the cold air was wearing on him, as was Luke's growing aggression.

THE LAST RAYS of sunlight bathed the living room in a warm, pink hue. Luke's head rested in Jimmy's lap on the couch as he twirled one of the strings that dangled down from Jimmy's hoodie. Dinner was both prepared and eaten in haste. The trip into the city had taken its toll on their empty stomachs, leaving little desire to pause in admiration of the home-cooked meal. After the sprint to the finish line, they crashed on the couch, their bellies now uncomfortably filled, hints of the steamed green vegetable still lingering on their breath. The muffled sounds of his neighbor's TV seeped through the walls, providing ambiance to their conversation.

"Was it lonely?" Luke asked, questioning Jimmy about his childhood.

"Sometimes. I always wanted a brother or sister. I think the idea of it seemed exciting, but I was close to my parents. They were enough."

"It's not always all it's cracked up to be," Luke replied. "I hated my sister, growing up. It wasn't until she went away to college that we actually became friends."

"But now you guys are close?" Jimmy asked as he combed his fingers through Luke's hair.

"Oh, yeah. I talk to her just about every day. Well, I did—before you."

Jimmy smiled. "She must hate me for hogging all your time."

"Trust me. I've heard it from her."

"Really?" Jimmy asked, anxious to know what Luke's sister thought of their current situation. "What did she say?"

"She just warned me. Says I should be careful."

"Careful? What is she worried about? Does she not like me? She hasn't even met me."

"She thinks I might be *in too deep*," Luke quoted.

Jimmy looked away for a moment, Luke's words penetrating. He wondered what Luke had told his sister, what he had said to ignite her concern. Her warning seemed to imply a one-sidedness, a disproportionate balance of affections.

"Do *you* think you're in too deep?" Jimmy asked.

"Nah, how could I be? We're just hanging out, right?" Luke asked, the question wet with unspoken frustration.

Jimmy flinched, suddenly under attack. He had been against labeling their relationship, but certainly not for lack of affection.

"You know we're more than just hanging out," Jimmy replied.

"Hey, I'm just repeating what you said."

Years ago, Jimmy had wanted nothing more than to call Luke his own. Now that he could, he hesitated. The past two months spent together had provided a break from his usual neurosis, a chance to live freely. Luke made it easy to just be. Jimmy savored their moments together without fear or concern, without analyzing what it meant and where it was going. Freedom was intoxicating. He had only ever tasted it before in small, fleeting doses. Now, he basked in it and wanted nothing to ruin it. He had no desire to assess what was going on, to define it concretely and get caught up in his head again. He only wished to enjoy it. But the weight of their significance could not be ignored and Luke seemed eager to acknowledge it.

"We both know we're on the same page," Jimmy began. "Why does it matter how we define it?"

"I'm not saying it does," Luke replied, backing down.

"It's not that I don't want to call you my boyfriend. I think I just don't like the word."

"So instead you just introduce me as your friend—like I'm no different than Charlie or Blake."

Jimmy sighed, surprised to discover just how much the issue had bothered Luke. His palm fell on Luke's forehead, and his thumb grazed the heavy bridge above Luke's eyes. The last thing he wanted was for his boyfriend to question how he felt. Jimmy had assumed it was self-evident. But perhaps Luke had no way of knowing that Jimmy's breath still shortened when they kissed. It seemed he was unaware of the knot that still formed in Jimmy's stomach when Luke smiled and laughed and held him.

"Did you pluck your eyebrows?" Jimmy asked, noticing a few missing hairs.

Luke grinned. "Sort of. I started to, but it hurt so I stopped."

Jimmy burst into laughter. It was a stretch to imagine Luke in front of his bathroom mirror, tweezers in hand.

"They're too big and bushy," Luke continued. "I've always hated them." Jimmy's amusement grew. Luke tugged at the strings of his hoodie, pulling Jimmy's face close to his. "Stop making fun of me."

"Okay, okay," Jimmy surrendered, kissing Luke as a peace offering. He grabbed Luke's face. "But don't fuck with your eyebrows. I love their bushiness." Jimmy pecked Luke's lips once more. "Move over."

Luke adjusted himself, slithering onto his side.

Jimmy fell into the space behind him and draped his arm across. "So what exactly should I call you? *Boyfriend—*" He auditioned the word, his mouth close to Luke's ear. "Sounds a little trite, don't you think?"

"Maybe, but what's the alternative? I hate *partner*."

"Definitely not. *Lover*," Jimmy suggested.

"Oh, please," Luke replied. "Even worse. Sounds like we're having an affair or something. Let's not worry about it. You're just my James."

"Your James," Jimmy repeated, letting the resonance of the words coupled together ring out for a moment. It was a title he would wear proudly. "I guess that makes you my Luke."

"Yes, it does."

Chapter Ten

WHEN JIMMY FIRST told his mother about Luke, he fired off the details as quickly and vaguely as possible. While the unease previously surrounding his sexuality had long-since been settled, there was little precedence with regards to the actuality of the matter. Being gay had, until now, been merely conceptual to his family. His mother and father were unaware of his nights out with Charlie and Blake, his fleeting escapades with strangers. They were, in most ways, completely oblivious to his life as a gay man. He shuddered to think how they would handle seeing it face-to-face.

"I don't know how this is going to go," he warned Luke, preparing him for the worst. "My parents are wonderful people and I love them dearly, but I imagine it might be awkward, probably a lot of silent moments. But don't try to fill it with unnecessary talk. Small talk is okay, but don't feel like you have to alleviate the tension." He was hard at work fighting with his belt, struggling to stab the metal clasp into a hole that didn't exist. "I think it's best if we just let it be, give them time to soak it all in. I'm sure, after this first visit, it will be easier. It's just going to take some time."

"I think you're overreacting." Luke reached down to help him, gracefully taking over the task at hand. "I'm sure it's going to be fine. Your mother sounds lovely. We have talked already, remember?"

"A thirty-second phone conversation hardly counts."

"It's obvious how much they love you. Trust me, I'm sure they are going to be nothing but happy."

"I know. I know they are, conceptually. But it's different, you know, when you have to actually deal with it."

"Deal with what?" Luke made his way to the dresser and pulled a shirt from the top drawer.

"They've never seen me with another guy before. I just think it's going to be a bit of an adjustment." Jimmy approached the low-hanging mirror near the closet and bent down as he adjusted his hair. "I don't want to shove it in their face or anything."

"I don't plan on blowing you in the middle of dinner."

Jimmy glared. "We should definitely hold back on any affection."

"Right, so I should just act like your roommate."

"Exactly."

Luke glared. "Fine. I'll keep my hands to myself," he promised as he buttoned up his shirt.

Jimmy took notice of Luke's frumpy plaid shirt.

"So you're wearing that?" he asked.

"Well, yeah. It's what I have on." Luke waited. "What? What's wrong with it?"

"It's ten sizes too big."

"No it's not!" Luke peered down at himself, tugging at the fabric to assess the amount of extra space.

"I could fit in there," Jimmy added. "You know you buy your clothes too big, right?"

"I like to be comfortable."

"Comfort is one thing; that's not what's going on there."

"I'm sorry I don't get my Burberry shirts tailored at Barney's like some people."

"Don't be an asshole. That was one shirt. And it was a birthday present to myself. You know that."

Luke shook his head, sighing as his arms dropped lifeless to his sides. "Well, give me one of yours then."

"I don't know if that gut is going to fit in one of mine," Jimmy replied with a chuckle.

"You little shit."

Jimmy opened the closet and studied his options. He sifted through the neatly organized row of button-downs as Luke approached, shirtless and waiting, pushing his gut out as he rubbed the shiny, hairless mound.

"Got it!" Jimmy exclaimed as he pulled out a firmly pressed blue oxford. He raised the hanging garment forward as he presented it to Luke.

"Really?" Luke asked, nearly cringing.

"What? It's very nice."

"Yeah, for a sixty-year-old Republican."

"Oh, please. It's classic."

"When have you ever worn that?" Luke asked.

"I don't think I have actually." Jimmy ran his hand along the collar and seams until he stumbled on a neatly bound collection of tags. "Nope. Still has the tags."

Luke pulled the shirt from the hanger and heaved and puffed as he thrust it on his bare torso and buttoned it up. It fit snug around his stomach, which had grown marginally during the passing months. The change was barely perceptible, but Jimmy enjoyed the tiny bit of extra padding. There was something about the new hint of thickness that begged to be grabbed. In truth, Luke would never face any real issues of weight gain. His slender frame could not support it. What developed was nothing more than a slight roundness to his overall build, the harsh angles of his skeletal figure somewhat softened by added flesh.

Jimmy approached, examining Luke closely. His hands glided across Luke's shoulders, down his arms like a tailor assessing the fit. He pressed Luke's belly, laughing at his own joke as he tried to compress the bump. Luke glared. Jimmy chuckled, wrapped his arms around, and grabbed Luke's ass. His khakis fit tight around the firm mound whose rise had grown more pronounced in recent months.

"See, look how nice you look," Jimmy affirmed.

"I barely fit in this thing," Luke sulked, his head resting on Jimmy's shoulder.

"Whaddya talk? It looks great. This, my friend, is how a shirt is meant to fit."

"My gut really is sticking out." Luke sighed in frustration.

"Pretty soon it's gonna roll over your belt," Jimmy added.

"Fuck off." Luke winced as he peeled himself away and moved to the bed. His thicker-than-usual ass sank into the edge of the mattress as he grabbed at his stomach, pushing and pulling as if hoping to manipulate its shape in some lasting way.

"Oh, come on," Jimmy sighed. "I'm kidding."

"I've got dad-bod already and I'm not even thirty," Luke lamented. "Pretty soon I'm going to be one of those old guys who has to bend over to see his dick when he pees."

Jimmy laughed as he took a seat near Luke. "Don't worry. I can hold your dick for you."

"I'm serious. I'm getting gross, aren't I?"

"You're being ridiculous. You gained like, two whole pounds. You couldn't get gross if you tried. Besides, I love you just the way you are. Beer belly and all."

"I need to start working out again. Did you just say you love me?" Luke asked.

Jimmy retraced his steps. "I guess I did."

Luke's grin bloomed, brightening his face. "So, you love me?"

"I guess I do," Jimmy replied.

"You guess?"

"Of course I do."

"Even with the beer belly?"

"Honestly, I don't think I've ever been more turned on by you," Jimmy admitted as he held Luke's face, lightly pecking his pouty lips. "This whole thing is really doing it for me."

"Oh is it?" Luke asked as he drew closer. "And what is it about this whole thing that you like?"

"More to grab onto," Jimmy replied as he took hold of Luke's hips. Their lips locked as they fell onto the bed. Jimmy wrapped his arms under Luke's, pulling him closer as he breathed him in. Their legs intertwined. He bit at Luke's bottom lip. "You look far better in this shirt than I ever could," he whispered.

Luke laughed, pressing his forehead against Jimmy's.

"Sorry to make such a fuss over everything," Jimmy apologized. "I'm just nervous."

"It's okay. I get it."

"I barely ever had friends over as a kid. So it's all a little much for me, I guess."

"Are you worried they won't like me?" Luke asked.

"Of course not. Everyone likes you."

"So then what is there to worry about?"

"I just hope they like *us*," Jimmy replied. "Because I like us. And I want them to like us too."

"I have a feeling they're going to like us," Luke affirmed with a knowing smile. "We are, after all, very likeable."

THEY RUSHED OUT of the train station, buried in cumbersome coats, and scurried toward Jimmy's father who was waiting in the nearly empty parking lot. Harvey's arms were crossed, his thin jacket billowing in the wind, as he braced against the old Subaru wagon. Luke swallowed hard at the sight of him as they approached. Harvey's build was average, but his towering stature could be intimidating. His resting face was stern, only sharpened by the cold Long Island air.

"It's about time," he shouted as Jimmy and Luke arrived. Jimmy was quick to explain that the train had been stalled on its way out of the city because of some technical difficulty. "I'm just giving you a hard time," Harvey confessed with a smile, his expression softening. He reached out and hugged Jimmy. "It's good to see you, kiddo. And this must be Luke."

Luke extended his hand as Harvey rushed in, hugging him tightly. Luke struggled to free his arms so that he might return the gesture, but Harvey's strong grip prevailed.

"Get in the car," Harvey commanded as he freed Luke. "It's freezing out."

When they pulled up to the house, only moments later, Malena was standing outside with her hands perched on her hips. Harvey pulled into the driveway and swung open his door.

"What's wrong?" he asked, confused by his wife's troubled expression.

"Pluto got away from me chasing after some cat. Now I can't get him back inside," she answered, shivering. "Hi, honey!" she exclaimed as Jimmy and Luke exited the car.

"Get inside," Harvey insisted. "I'll get the dog."

Jimmy rushed toward his mother and hugged her. "Mom, you're freezing."

"That dog." Malena let go of Jimmy and geared her attention toward the boy smiling politely at Jimmy's side. "So this is Luke," she said, eyeing him up for a moment before extending her arms.

Malena's voice was soft and sincere, its cool disposition rarely displaced. When she did speak sternly, she commanded attention, but Jimmy could count on one hand the number of times he remembered seeing her boil up. His father's speech was far more blunt and to the point. It was through Harvey's actions, the tightness of his hugs, the way his nose crinkled when he smiled at Jimmy, that he expressed his softer side.

Luke seemed at ease as he entered the house. Jimmy's parents were instantly warm and welcoming, escorting him through the neatly decorated living room to the kitchen where steam rose from noisy pots and pans. The countertop was filled with remnants of ingredients that had made their way onto the stove. Malena hustled to clear the counter, tossing dirty dishes and cutting boards in the sink, sweeping away scraps of broccoli with her bare hands.

"Leave it for later," Harvey said, turning off the stove as he signaled Jimmy to set the table.

Malena was eager to learn about Luke's family during dinner. She asked what his mother and father did, where they were originally from, how long they had been married. Jimmy listened, absorbing details he hadn't thought to discover for himself. Harvey interjected once in a while, mostly to offer his approval. "Textiles," he said. "That's a good business to be in."

Luke was gracious and well-spoken as he always was. Jimmy watched, pleasantly surprised, as the two worlds converged.

"We're happy to finally meet you," Malena said to Luke as she twirled a string of pasta around her fork. "Jimmy's been keeping you away from us on purpose," she added.

Jimmy denied his mother's claim with a glare as he chewed.

"Probably worried I'd make a fool of myself in front of you guys," Luke replied.

"Hardly," Harvey said. "I'm sure he's worried we'll embarrass him."

Jimmy rolled his eyes, his mouth too full to reply.

"How are we doing?" Harvey asked. "Not prying too much?"

"Not at all," Jimmy replied as he wiped his mouth clean. "I'm learning a lot actually," he added, turning his attention to Luke. "I didn't know your dad worked in India."

"Not exclusively," Luke replied. "But he's there at least a couple of times every year. It's still their main supplier."

"Jimmy's always wanted to go to India," Malena added with a smile.

"Really?" Luke asked. "I didn't know that."

"It was a long time ago," Jimmy replied, slightly sinking in his chair.

Harvey was quick to explain how determined Jimmy was to experience the land of saints and sages when he was younger. "He even found a summer exchange program that he insisted we let him join."

Luke listened, wide-eyed and eager to learn all the details of Jimmy's childhood dream.

"We so badly wanted to agree," Malena added, "but I just couldn't send him so far away all by himself."

"I would've been fine," Jimmy murmured under his breath.

"You were only fifteen," Harvey interjected. "It was too risky."

"He wanted it so badly," Malena remembered. "It broke my heart to say no."

"Well, maybe we can go together," Luke suggested.

"There you go!" Harvey exclaimed. "Now you've got someone to watch out for you."

Jimmy flinched at his father's excitement, his temperature rising as his mother also agreed. Suddenly, India seemed like a good idea. What was once dismissed was now being unanimously supported, now that Luke was in the picture.

"I could have my dad arrange everything for us." Luke jumped into planning mode, discussing where they might go and what they might see, Malena and Harvey nodding in support like cheerleaders on the sidelines.

Jimmy stayed quiet, smiling as best he could, suppressing the urge to retaliate. India was meant to be a chance to see the world, explore new things, grow as an individual. He had always imagined trekking on trains and crowded buses on his own, paving the way for new discoveries independent of any caretaker. Surely, he would enjoy sharing the experience with the man he loved, but he grew squeamish at the idea that Luke was somehow a requirement, a necessary chaperone. Did the life he had built for himself before Luke suddenly mean nothing? Was it not proof enough to his doubtful parents that he was capable of standing on his own two feet?

"We'd probably need to go back another time to see the south," Luke continued. "I've heard it can be overwhelming to do it all at once. We may want to pace ourselves instead of packing in too much."

"I'm so happy you'll finally have a chance to go." Malena smiled at Jimmy. "You boys will need to leave us all the information about where you'll be staying, so we can keep track of where you are. Make sure you're all right."

Luke squeezed Jimmy's hand, seemingly pleased to have his plans approved.

Jimmy quickly pulled away. "Why have you never gone before?" he asked Luke. "With your dad."

"I guess I never really gave it much thought. It was just his job." Luke looked at Jimmy inquisitively, seemingly aware that something was amiss.

Jimmy's expression softened. "It's a thought," he uttered with feigned enthusiasm. "Depends on if I can take time off work."

After dinner, they moved to the living room. Harvey mixed drinks for the boys, eager to show off his newfound hobby. "I was never much of a drinker," he told Luke, "but Malena and I were at a friend's house for their anniversary party and they hired a bartender—well, I guess technically he's a mixologist."

"It was an impressive party," Malena chimed in. "They hired waiters and a DJ. There was even a tiny dance floor with strobe lights. It was a very fun night."

Jimmy cringed at the idea of his parents at a party with a mixologist and DJ. *Who are these friends?* he wondered.

"So the mixologist started giving a sort of informal lesson on how to make an old fashioned," Harvey continued. "It got me thinking I could do more. The next day I started researching drinks online and got to work. Lately I've been experimenting with my own concoctions. It's been a lot of fun."

"I can't complain," Malena said, giggling. "It gives me an excuse for an after-dinner drink every night."

"And that's after the glass of wine she has *with* dinner," Harvey added.

Jimmy watched, shocked and bewildered, his eyes darting back and forth between an amused Luke and his giddy parents. Who were these people? Certainly not the parents Jimmy grew up with. They were suddenly attending trendy Long Island house parties and having drinks every night, cracking jokes like they were already drunk. They seemed only minutes away from pulling out a joint.

"Wow," Luke said, wincing after his first sip. "That's a sharp flavor."

"My own take on a Manhattan," Harvey replied with confidence.

Jimmy took a small, timid sip and cringed. He rested the glass on the coffee table. "The new table looks great," he said, rubbing his hands against the cold, white marble top.

"We just listened to what you suggested," Malena replied. "Jimmy's our design expert," she said to Luke. "We hardly do anything in the house without consulting him first."

Luke turned to Jimmy with a grin. "Really?"

"The living room was all his idea," Harvey mentioned as he took a seat on the couch near his wife. "We had this brown tile at first. He had us put in wood flooring, which I think looks great."

"And the sofa set," Malena added. "He was very unhappy with our sofas."

Luke chuckled. "Was he? What was so wrong with your sofas?"

"Too big and bulky," Harvey answered.

"We had to buy new ones once we finished the floors."

"Honestly, I didn't see the need at first, but the new ones really do make a difference," Harvey said as he ran his hand across the chair arm. "I would have never picked them out myself, but James has an eye for these things."

"Everyone that comes over is always very impressed," Malena explained.

Jimmy sank into the new, sleek sofa. Its low, firm back didn't offer much in the way of comfort, but it certainly looked nice.

"One of the perks of having a gay son," Luke murmured under his breath, unable to restrain a quiet laugh.

Harvey chuckled. Malena laughed. She took a swig of the pink drink and glanced over to Jimmy, noticing his discomfort.

"Jimmy's always been good at everything he tries," she offered.

Malena went on to describe Jimmy's many childhood endeavors, reliving the many times he redecorated his bedroom, changing color schemes and arrangements with an unquenchable zest for perfection. She described the musical instruments he had tried to learn, the artwork that won awards in school, the short films he made as a teenager, upping Jimmy's credibility. Luke listened attentively.

"Piano was my favorite," Harvey announced. "We enjoyed listening to him practice every afternoon."

"You play piano?" Luke asked excitedly.

"No," Jimmy replied. "I only ever learned two songs."

"But you played them so well," Harvey continued.

"You'll have to play them for me sometime," Luke said with a grin. He rested his hand on Jimmy's twitching leg and squeezed it playfully.

Jimmy's leg froze. His body stiffened as he glanced over to see if his parents had seen the inappropriate sign of affection. He sat up, adjusting himself on the sofa as he tried to wiggle his way out of Luke's grasp. Luke's hand followed, glued to Jimmy's thigh.

Malena looked to Jimmy. "You should show Luke the rest of the house," she suggested as if she could detect her son's discomfort. "I left an extra set of towels in the room for you, dear," she said to Luke. "You boys make yourselves comfortable. We're going to settle in."

"It's barely ten," Jimmy replied.

"We're old," Harvey added as he rose, collecting the glasses and leaving them near the bar, suddenly eager to give Luke and Jimmy their space.

"Where should we sleep?" Jimmy asked.

Malena looked at Jimmy. "In your room. Where else would you sleep?"

"But should we both—"

"There's more than enough space up there for the both of you," Malena interjected. "You know where to find extra blankets if you need it, but your dad's got the heat cranked up as usual so I'm sure you'll be fine."

LUKE ENTERED JIMMY'S bedroom with a skip in his step. Jimmy quietly closed the door behind him.

"Here we are," Luke proclaimed, arms spread wide as if displaying the room to an audience. "Where it all began for young James. This is kinda magical, really." He wandered around the room, assessing every square inch of the space, studying the few perfectly aligned posters on the walls, the figurines on the wooden shelf above Jimmy's small, corner desk. "This is where little Jimmy grew up."

"Sort of," Jimmy replied. "It's not like I haven't been back here regularly. I don't still have my NASCAR bedspread or anything."

"You had a NASCAR bedspread?" Luke asked.

"Not by choice."

"Obviously not."

Jimmy took a seat at the edge of his bed, covered with a nondescript, navy-blue comforter.

"Sorry there aren't more clues to my childhood buried in here. You'll have to keep extracting those from my parents, I guess."

"They are amazing, by the way. I'm actually jealous of you. This has been a perfect night."

Jimmy grew quiet for a moment, seeing the evening through Luke's eyes. "It has been pretty perfect."

Luke examined the small row of books covered in dust, tucked away on a shelf near the bedroom window. Jimmy questioned for a moment what might be hidden away there, but it was useless to entertain such worries. There was no longer anything to hide from Luke, who had so effortlessly squeezed himself into the family.

"Also, your dad is an amazing cook," Luke continued. "I see where you get your know-how in the kitchen from. But his cocktails," he grimaced. "Not so sure about that Manhattan."

An unsettling discomfort filled Jimmy. His childhood self returned, insisting to regain its place as commander-in-chief, unwilling to resign its authority to some naïve newcomer. A suffocating worry, familiar but distant, loomed over Jimmy, that stifling fear that accompanied the onset of any major change or shift in life. Suddenly Luke was cracking jokes with his father, taking care of him in India, rendering him a mere accessory in his own home with his own family.

"Are you okay?" Luke asked as he approached, taking a seat on the bed near Jimmy.

"Yeah. Of course. Why?"

"You've been a little distracted most of the night."

"Maybe too much pasta," Jimmy replied as he threw his back down on the bed, commanding his mind to stop ruining what really had been a perfect night.

Luke followed, falling next to Jimmy. "See. I told you," he said, his attention geared toward the glow-in-the-dark stars pasted on the ceiling. "It all worked out perfectly."

"I'm glad you guys are getting along. You're having an okay time?" Jimmy asked.

Luke chuckled. "I wish we could trade parents. I don't feel half as comfortable around my own. How come you never told me you want to visit India?"

"I don't know. It never came up. Besides, it was another lifetime ago. I haven't thought about all that in a while."

"You still want to go?"

"I guess."

"Would you want to go with me?" Luke asked.

"Of course," Jimmy replied, turning to face Luke whose hands were clasped at his chest, his fingers tapping rhythmically to a song only he could hear. Jimmy stared in admiration at the boy who was now his home, resting comfortably in a world that was once only his. "You look nice in my shirt."

"I think I felt a button pop during dinner."

Jimmy ran his hand across Luke. "No, seems like they're all still there."

Luke turned to his side. His gaze met Jimmy's. "You sure you're okay?"

"Yes," Jimmy replied. "I'm more than okay."

"Why so quiet, then?"

"Just pensive, I guess."

"I'm sorry if I was too familiar or something."

"No. I'm glad you guys are getting along. I hope things go this well when I meet your folks."

"Don't expect this," Luke replied. "My parents are good people, but we're not nearly as close and open with each other as you guys are."

"I can understand that. Everyone's dynamic is different."

"I never felt like I could really talk to them growing up. They're so closed off. We were all just polite to each other, but never particularly loving."

"Explains a lot," Jimmy replied.

"Hey," Luke protested, tugging at Jimmy's shirt. "I never hold back my affection with you."

"I do recall saying I love you earlier today. You have yet to reply."

"Did I not?"

"Nope."

"I think I replied."

Jimmy inched closer and began to caress Luke's chest. The remnants of his cologne had mixed with sweat giving him that sharp end-of-day flavor Jimmy enjoyed so much. He breathed it in as he kissed Luke, allowing his lips to stay pressed comfortably against Luke's for some time.

Luke's hand worked its way up Jimmy's torso, landing on his face where it rested. Jimmy twitched. His body had a way of responding instantly to Luke's touch.

"We probably shouldn't do anything, right?" Jimmy asked. "It feels weird, don't you think?"

"Yeah. You're probably right," Luke whispered. "It'd be kinda disrespectful."

Their lips moved slowly in and out of each other's embrace, gaining traction as they progressed. Jimmy mounted Luke, trying not to disrupt the fragile springs in the mattress as he carefully removed his pants. He unfastened Luke's belt with a chuckle. "We'll be really quiet," he whispered.

Luke grinned.

They worked judiciously, Jimmy straddling Luke, trying his best to quiet his growing satisfaction. Despite their carefulness, the bed squealed as their momentum hastened. Jimmy leaned forward, hoping to slow things down, but his head went crashing into the bedhead. Luke burst into laughter. Jimmy covered his mouth as he rose and fell more cautiously, his face hovering over Luke until they finished, erupting with muted moans and gasps.

Luke kissed Jimmy as he rose. "I think I'm gonna shower," he said. "I'm all sweaty and sticky."

Jimmy nodded, out of breath. He fell on to the bed as Luke tiptoed away wearing only his shirt, his bare ass in plain sight.

"Wait," Jimmy whispered, hoping to convince Luke to at least put on his boxers before leaving the room, but Luke was quick to exit, closing the door before scurrying across the hallway. Jimmy grew relieved once he heard the bathroom door close and the water run. He caught his breath and sat up against the headboard, spreading his legs out across the bed. The heat was blaring. It felt like summer in the bedroom. Suddenly, he heard the wood floors creak. The sound grew louder as footsteps approached. Jimmy sprang out of bed, searching frantically for his boxers. He rummaged under the sheets and peered under the bed, finally finding his underwear resting on the night table's edge. He thrust them on and buried himself under the covers as he watched the door in fear, anxiously waiting for his mother to burst open the door and enter the room, which wreaked of sex and sweat. A minute passed as he lay frozen. The floors quieted. Finally, he heard a door close in the distance. His parents were likely settling in. They must have known better than to disturb him and Luke.

Jimmy relaxed, rolled to his side, and freed his legs from the warm comforter. His parents' nonchalance regarding the entire evening had been unexpected, to say the least. It was shocking how easy it was to have sex in his childhood bed with his mother and father across the hall. Jimmy wondered if they suspected what was going on. Perhaps they had heard the quiet whispers and moans as their son bounced up and down in delight.

His mom had cleaned the room. The heap of boxes usually stored in the corner was now gone. The closet doors, usually hanging off their tracks, were perfectly aligned and sealed shut. Jimmy wondered how often he might return now that he was busy living his own life. His parents hardly seemed to mind his absence. It seemed, instead, to provide them with a newfound independence—a chance to learn to make cocktails and enjoy the occasional dance party.

The door opened as Luke crept in, his hand coyly covering his bare crotch. He placed the folded shirt on the chest of drawers as he shut the door.

"What are you doing walking around naked?" Jimmy asked.

"I didn't exactly think this through," Luke whispered as he tiptoed toward the bed, a silent grin stretched across his face, his dick now flapping around freely. Jimmy smiled as he opened the covers, making room for him. Luke slipped in with ease as Jimmy turned to his other side and pressed his back snuggly against Luke's chest.

"Your hair's still wet." Jimmy pushed strands of it out of his face as they settled in.

"It'll dry."

Luke wrapped his arm tightly around Jimmy. The smell of soap still lingered on his clean skin. Jimmy longed to devour him all over again as he pressed closer. Instead, he settled for pecking at Luke's arm.

"That picture in the bathroom of you and your dad when you were little is so cute," Luke whispered. "But a little weird."

"How so?"

"Why is it in the bathroom?" Luke asked, giggling softly in Jimmy's ear. "I felt weird wiping my dick dry with little Jimmy watching."

Jimmy chuckled. "Trust me, little Jimmy was probably thrilled to see it."

"Wanna have another go at it?" Luke asked as he pressed his bare dick against Jimmy.

"Go to sleep," Jimmy commanded.

"All right, fine. Be that way," Luke said as he adjusted his head to rest more comfortably near Jimmy's. "Love you. Good night."

"Finally!"

"Just wanted to make you sweat a little."

"Fucker," Jimmy rammed his elbow into Luke's stomach.

Luke flinched. "So who's gonna turn off the light?"

Chapter Eleven

JIMMY HAD GROWN accustomed to spending countless late nights in the office since becoming a project manager. Most days, the promotion kept him pinned to his desk as one hour rolled into the next, night creeping up on him unexpectedly. It didn't bother him much while in the thick of it. It was only during the moments between tasks when he stopped to wonder what free time might feel like that he felt the burden of being overworked. But he had no desire to let down Michael, who had entrusted him with a hefty workload as new clients filled the company's roster. Late-night texts from his boss and weekend visits to the office had become the norm. The pressure to stay on top of everything was sometimes stifling, but even in the midst of the added stress, a sense of purpose fueled Jimmy, making the juggling act well worth it. He did, however, find himself canceling on Luke more often than not.

Luke remained supportive, but his growing agitation was becoming harder to hide. He joked about Michael's intentions, creating an imagined affair that over time became less a joke and more a genuine concern. Luke's body retracted whenever Michael got in the way of his time with Jimmy, his breath shortened. Jimmy brushed it off. Though it had once been a fantasy of his own, those days were long behind him. He did, however, regret his growing absence. Even when with Luke, he was preoccupied, constantly checking his phone and answering emails.

In an effort to make up for his guilt, Jimmy had given Luke a key to his place so that he might come and go as he pleased, independent of Jimmy's unpredictable schedule. Luke became a fixture in Jimmy's apartment. Most nights Jimmy returned home to find him spread out on the couch, the TV blaring, the pungent smell of pot filling the living room. It, at times, bothered Jimmy. He sometimes missed having a quiet, clean apartment to come home to after a long day at the office. But most often, he surrendered to the state of things, slipping into the couch with ease.

Tonight, he had hoped to leave early, maybe even make dinner and have some time to unwind. The workload seemed light earlier in the morning, but the afternoon got the best of him. Before he knew it, day settled into night and his hopes of making it home at a reasonable hour vanished.

"Why don't you take off," Michael suggested as he emerged from his office. "I can handle the rest on my own." His shirt was untucked, wrinkled along the edges. His eyes sat heavy on his tired face.

"Are you sure?" Jimmy asked, hopeful.

"Yes, go. I'm just waiting on the final set of revisions from Mark. I can send them out on my own."

"Don't stay too late," Jimmy replied. "I can always send it out in the morning. With the time difference, we'll still make it."

Michael agreed with a nod as he shuffled back to his office.

Jimmy gathered his things, looking back at his colleague before entering the elevator. It was not the same Michael he had desired a lifetime ago—the dapper man, whose appearance was nothing if not flawless. He seemed aloof now, his mind always in two places at once, his eyes glazed over, lacking the presence he once possessed. Jimmy worried his future might look similar. He had always looked up to Michael, aspired to be like him, but not this version of the man, perpetually overworked and drained of life.

He dialed Luke as soon as the doors to the elevator opened to the empty downstairs lobby. He had promised to check in earlier.

"I'm sorry. I really thought tonight would be an early one. Where are you?"

"I'm at my place," Luke answered, sleep weighing heavy on his voice. "I figured you'd be late."

"Did you eat?"

"I ate with Doug after work."

"Okay, well, maybe tomorrow night? We can go out. You okay?"

"Yeah, I'm fine. Just tired. I had a beer with dinner, so I'm kinda out for the night."

"I'm beat too. Probably just going to hit the bed as soon as I get home."

"You should get a car; it's late. Love you."

The air was still as Jimmy walked across Nineteenth Street, heading for the subway. A glimmer of excitement fueled his stride as he imagined taking a long shower and cozying up with a book, but Luke's disappointment echoed in his ears and guilt returned. It was surprisingly pleasant out, the perfect blend of warmth and crisp coolness. The city had been granted a burst of spring. He unbuttoned his coat and slowed his pace, the weather too good to waste. As he walked along the nearly empty sidewalks, Jimmy wondered what a night like this would have looked like a few months ago, before there was Luke. Nowadays, free time was no longer his own. It had to be rationed and shared. He was bound to always be concerned about someone else's feelings and desires. At times, Jimmy missed the privileges only solitude could provide. He had learned to live alone so well that the need for anything else dissipated over time. He had, in many ways, mastered the art of being alone. But life presented him with a new way of being, one he was still working to figure out. His fear, as it settled in deeper and deeper with each passing month, was that he might lose that self-sufficient, unattached version of himself—that he might forget what it was to be happy on his own.

In his previous life, Jimmy enjoyed wandering around Manhattan without a definite goal in mind. He decided he might allow himself to do so tonight, at least for a little while. The city provided the perfect arena for drifters with no agenda. He once reveled in walking through the ever-changing neighborhoods of the city, the characteristics of one replaced by another, each with its own singular charm. The chaotic sights and smells of Chinatown had led him to Little Italy and farther into SoHo whose cobblestone streets and pre-war architecture sent his imagination soaring with dreams of future vastness. He would often head east to walk along the long row of bars and restaurants of the Lower East Side, passing parks and basketball courts, walls covered in graffiti, the entire neighborhood drenched from top to bottom in an endless array of colors and sounds.

It was not uncommon to spend entire days wandering, absorbing every drop of the world around him, feeling full and content upon returning home. But there was also an undeniable hint of sadness to his old ritual. It would be naive to forget that tiny bit of truth. His thoughts as they flowed from one vision to the next during his aimless walks most often landed on his long-lasting state of loneliness, his inability to find anyone with whom he could share a piece of his wonder. It was the remembrance of that tiny morsel of sadness that thrust him into an intellectual merry-go-round, coming up with new reasons as to why the universe had fated him to forever remain an observer, devising plans to change his destiny.

Now he walked through Union Square with his head held high as he passed the lonely laggards of the night. There was no longer a need to dream up a future with some passing stranger, to imagine a romance that didn't exist. He had found someone. Not just anyone, but a man plucked from those very daydreams. He had somehow gained a place in the partnered-up world around him, unknowingly veering off the lonely road he once expertly traveled, slipping into a reality he only ever imagined. His life became part of that universal chain of connected people, attaching itself to the whole with an inherent sense of know-how.

He took a seat on the stone wall along the park's perimeter, deciding to enjoy the night's stillness, taking pleasure in the return to solitude, a state of being that both plagued him and served as home. He shuddered to consider being alone, *home*, but it did feel nice. As much as he appreciated the new life he was building, moments arose, despite his best efforts to keep them at bay, when he felt like a stranger in a foreign land wearing the clothes of the natives well enough to pass as one, but silently aware of his costume's frayed edges, waiting for the seams to rip and the threads to unravel. Perhaps, he decided in an effort to end the mental tug-of-war, there was room for both. Maybe having one did not require losing the other. He promised himself as he leapt off the wall that he would try and find more alone time—more time to wander and think and dream. Luke would undoubtedly understand. There was, after all, no harm in spending time alone. Surely he could have his cake and eat it too.

Chapter Twelve

JIMMY'S CHEEK LAY glued to Luke's sweaty chest, his breathing finally slowing to a normal pace.

"The heat's too high," he mumbled.

"It's just our lovemaking steaming up the joint," Luke answered.

Jimmy's body ached, drained from hard work. He glided his hand across Luke's chest, which rose and fell. Luke drew circles on Jimmy's shoulder with his finger. Their sex life's recent slowdown had left them starving. Today, Jimmy was free from work and they wasted no time, devouring each other and resting only to continue again, sweat dripping from their bodies as they moved.

Jimmy's body opened to Luke. Luke controlled it with skill, pushing Jimmy to the edge of sometimes-unbearable pleasure. Luke had grown more commanding, often stopping Jimmy from finishing, pinning his arms down as he deviously toyed with him, allowing Jimmy the satisfaction of release only when he saw fit. It was exhilarating, a rush Jimmy had come to crave, especially now that there was rarely time to fully indulge.

"So, what are you going to do?" Jimmy asked, feeling slightly rejuvenated.

"What can I do? I have to find somewhere else to live."

"Are they even allowed to do that? Aren't there laws against that sort of thing?"

"It's not like they're kicking me out," Luke replied. "They're just not renewing my lease."

"Do they really think they can get more for that place?"

"I don't think they're renting it out again. Probably just going back to using it as a storage closet."

Jimmy raised his head, sitting up as a thought entered his mind. He hadn't planned on asking Luke to move in, but it did seem like the most obvious solution. He had, of course, entertained the idea before, but had always imagined it would occur farther down the road, when things were more settled at work and he could regain some semblance of a life. But now that his boyfriend was on the verge of being homeless, it seemed cruel not to bring it up.

Luke's face lit up at the mention of it.

"But would you want me here?" he asked. "All the time?"

"Of course!" Jimmy exclaimed, though as the words *all the time* rang in his ears he began to doubt himself. "You practically live here already."

"The thought had crossed my mind, but I didn't want to bring it up. Do you think it's too soon?"

"No," Jimmy replied. It began to feel more and more like a good idea. "I don't think it is. Do you?"

"It doesn't *feel* too soon."

"Exactly!" Jimmy sprang up from the bed, now sure of himself. He shuffled around the floor in search of his boxers as Luke chuckled. "Maybe it's crazy," Jimmy continued as he pulled up his boxers and returned to the bed. "But if it feels right, then it is! What else is there to consider? It's not like there's some sort of timeline we're supposed to stick to."

"Yeah!" Luke agreed as he sat up. "Why not?"

"Let's do this!"

"I'm moving to Queens!"

THE FOLLOWING WEEKEND, they filled a few small boxes with Luke's things—books and DVDs, his PlayStation and a handful of games. There wasn't much. His place was sparse, and he was adamant about only bringing the essentials, not wanting to burden Jimmy with unnecessary clutter. They parceled off the rest into categories of what would be thrown out and what could be donated—old board games, tired sweaters, unused ski gear for a trip upstate that never materialized.

"What are you going to do with the couch?" Jimmy asked as he lifted one of the torn cushions to find a collection of crumbs and loose change buried underneath. "You're not emotionally attached to it, are you? It's very comfortable and all, but—"

"Don't worry," Luke interrupted. "I wasn't planning on bringing it with me. Let's just take it out to the curb; someone will pick it up."

"Thank God. There's no way this thing was going to work in my place."

"*Our* place," Luke replied.

Jimmy walked up to Luke and buried his hands in the front pockets of his mustard-yellow hoodie. "Oh yes, of course—*our* place."

"I promise you still have reign over all things decor in *our* home, so don't worry." Luke grabbed a hold of Jimmy's ass, cupping it firmly. "Let's say we have a go on it one more time before it's too late."

"Never again. We might catch something just from being this close to it."

"You didn't seem to mind before."

THE COUCH'S WEIGHT matched its plushness. Jimmy and Luke struggled to lift it out of the tiny space and hoist it down the treacherous stairwell, scraping the walls on the way down. "At least I'm leaving my mark on the place," Luke joked. Jimmy smiled before fear took over.

"If I fall over these rails, it's a done deal," he said, peering down the narrow stairwell.

"You got it, just one step at a time. The elevator's straight ahead."

By the time they made it down to ground level, they were both painfully out of breath. Jimmy's shirt clung to his body, covered in sweat. He gasped for air as he let go of the robust mass of wood and fabric.

"You doing okay?" Luke asked.

"We should've just left it in there."

"I don't want to give them any reason to keep my deposit," Luke replied.

"I think I'm gonna pass out."

"I know. Me too. But hey, we made it."

"Not yet," Jimmy managed to utter as he pointed to the narrow lobby door. "Is it even going to fit?"

"I got it in here," Luke answered.

"I think we'll have to flip it and pull it out on its side."

"No, it'll fit. Why don't we switch spots so I can push from the back," Luke suggested as he leapt over the couch and landed near Jimmy.

"There's no way this is going to fit," Jimmy replied, exhaustion worsening his agitation. "Just look at it. It's wider than the doorway."

"Nothing a little brute force can't fix."

"You're going to take down the doorframe," Jimmy persisted.

Luke bent down and grabbed the couch from underneath with a heavy sigh. "Will you just trust me?"

"Why can't we just turn it over?" Jimmy insisted. "It would be way easier."

"Because we don't need to," Luke replied sharply, sweat dripping down his face as he readied for action. "It'll fit."

"Fine." Jimmy was too tired to argue. "If you say so."

Following Luke's lead, he climbed on to the couch and walked less agilely over the frumpy cushions before leaping into the doorway.

"Just guide it out," Luke directed. "I'll do the pushing from back here."

Jimmy pried the door open and held it in place with his foot as he tried to find a place for his hands to rest on the sides of the cumbersome sofa.

Luke thrust forward.

"Wait!" Jimmy screamed as the hefty mass charged toward him. It only moved a few inches, but it was enough to wedge his left hand between the doorframe and the couch. He cried out in pain as he yanked his arm back. It didn't budge. He tugged at it again, trying to free it with all his might as Luke struggled to pull the sofa out of the way. Jimmy made one final tug as the sofa retreated, grazing his hand against a protruding screw from the door hinge as he freed it, peeling a gash from his wrist to his knuckles. The pain of tearing flesh rushed through his body. A thin stream of blood began to pour, dripping on the concrete below. Jimmy looked down, forgetting his pain for a moment as he watched the red puddle form at his feet.

Luke shouted as he jumped over the sofa, rushing to Jimmy's side.

Jimmy stood frozen. His body numb.

Luke grabbed a hold of the wounded limb, thrust away his hoodie, peeled off his T-shirt, and wrapped the white cotton, drenched in sweat, around Jimmy's hand. He squeezed it tightly as he tied a large knot in Jimmy's palm.

"Fuck! Are you okay?" Luke's voice quivered with concern as he waited for a response from a motionless Jimmy.

"No, I'm not okay!" Jimmy shouted. "What the fuck!" The sharp sting of pain returned. It traveled like razors through his arm, jolting him back to awareness.

"We need to get this looked at," Luke said with terror in his eyes. "It looks really deep." He surveyed the street as if hoping to find a doctor surreptitiously passing at that very moment.

"I wasn't even ready!" Jimmy hollered. "Why did you start pushing?" His words echoed across the sidewalk.

"I'm so sorry, babe. It looks really deep." Luke fluttered around, shirtless, in full panic mode. "We need to get you to a doctor."

"I told you it wasn't going to fit!" Jimmy persisted. "But you insisted on being an asshole, and now I have a fucking hole in my hand."

"I know. I'm sorry. I didn't see your hand there."

"Of course you didn't. This is so typical."

"What is that supposed to mean?"

"Besides, even if by some stroke of magic this enormous piece of shit could fit, why would you just start pushing?" Jimmy winced between words, his pain only causing his voice to rise. "You never think things through. I didn't even have a chance to grab a hold of it. What was the big fucking rush?"

"Why didn't you hold the top and bottom?" Luke shouted back, in full defense mode, his voice as loud as Jimmy's. "Why would you grab the sides in the first place? That doesn't make any sense!"

"That's not the point!" Jimmy barked. "I didn't even have a chance to assess the situation."

"Assess the situation? It's not rocket science! I said, *just guide it out*."

"Which is what I was trying to do when suddenly a couch was coming at me!"

Just then, an elderly woman approached. "Are you okay, hon?" she asked, spotting the blood-soaked T-shirt dangling from Jimmy's hand.

"I'm fine. Thank you. We just had a bit of an accident."

She glanced over to Luke, shirtless and enraged. "I can see that. You really should get that taken care of. It could get infected."

Luke grabbed a hold of Jimmy's wounded hand as the woman continued on her way. "We have to get you to a doctor. It really could be infected."

Pain came rushing forward again, another sharp sting of agony. Jimmy's eyes filled as he screamed out, "Fuck! It hurts like hell."

Luke carefully raised Jimmy's arm. "Maybe you should keep it up," he suggested, his voice softer. "To stop the bleeding. I think it's pretty deep. You may need stitches." Luke held back his own tears as he watched them stream from Jimmy's eyes. Jimmy bit hard on his bottom lip, stilted breaths quieting as he gathered his composure.

"I don't need stitches," he replied. "Let's just move this fucking thing so I can go nurse my wounds."

"Fuck the couch," Luke barked. "We've got to get this looked at. I'm so sorry, babe."

Jimmy worked hard to silence the pain. "Let's move this thing first; then we can maybe get it looked at. I think it's not as bad as it looks."

"How? You've only got one working hand."

"Can you please just flip it? If it's on its side, you can just push it out on your own."

Luke agreed, this time without protesting. With the help of Jimmy's intact hand, they turned the couch on its side and thrust it out of the doorway and onto the sidewalk where they positioned it up against the light post.

Luke returned to Jimmy's side and unwrapped the blood-soaked T-shirt. The bleeding had lessened, though the pain was growing with each passing minute. Jimmy watched as Luke attended to the matter, careful not to touch the gash. The lines on his forehead scrunched together. His eyes filled with sorrow.

"It's cold out," Jimmy said. "And you don't even have a shirt on. Let's go inside."

They made their way back to the nearly empty apartment lined with boxes and organized clutter. Luke ushered Jimmy into the tiny bathroom where he dug through a shoebox resting on the bathtub's edge.

"I can at least clean it for now. I know I have some stuff in here somewhere."

He knelt down in front of Jimmy who sat on the rim of the tub. Jimmy's head rested against the cold, tile wall as Luke cleaned the wound with a ball of cotton, holding his hand and working with the softest tenderness. Jimmy watched, eyes half squinting. Numbness began to set in again helping to alleviate the pain.

"Looks like you know what you're doing," he told Luke.

"We still need to get it looked at."

"It doesn't look deep. I think it's fine," Jimmy replied.

"Don't be stubborn."

"Me? If you weren't being stubborn in the first place, none of this would've happened."

Luke sighed as he rubbed ointment across the cut, working it in carefully. "Maybe it doesn't need stitches," he admitted after examining it further. "But it's still safest to get it looked at."

The ointment cooled Jimmy's burning flesh. The razor-sharp sting of pain was slowly dissipating. "Is there an urgent care around? I know we're going to end up wasting the entire day in the waiting room for no reason."

Luke shook his head as he bandaged the wound. "We'll find one. They might lock me up for domestic abuse, though."

Jimmy laughed, eager to be amused, but a sliver of regret arose with his smile. It wasn't entirely Luke's fault. Perhaps he had been too harsh, but he had no desire to admit that just yet. Luke finished dressing the wound. His tongue poked out of his mouth as he worked, his attention keenly focused. He was careful to wrap it tightly. He sealed the bandages and patted it down, turning Jimmy's hand over to examine his work. When he was satisfied he rose and took Jimmy's free hand, ushering him off the tub's edge. "Let's just hope they don't have to cut it off," he joked.

Jimmy smiled. "I could probably manage with a hook."

Chapter Thirteen

DOUG'S BEARD WAS severe. The kind of shag that seemed more like a cry for attention than an earnest expression of personal style. Adding to the pretention was a loosely fitted beanie carelessly draped over his head, as though it had been unknowingly placed there, perfectly accidental. His jeans were torn up at the edges, his sneakers covered in a layer of dirt that made Jimmy cringe at the sight of them resting on his area rug.

Jimmy had returned home from yoga to find Luke and Doug on the couch staring at their respective laptop screens. He greeted them as he entered, welcoming Luke's friend with the forced etiquette he had grown accustomed to using, trying to mask his disappointment at the sight of the visitor in his home when all he wanted to do was return to a peaceful living room, cuddle up with a book, and allow the few hours left in the day to quietly drift away.

Jimmy hoped, as he emerged from the bathroom, showered and rejuvenated, that Doug might be gone, but to his further disappointment, they were still working, frozen in the same positions he had left them. Jimmy made his way to the kitchen, a noticeable heaviness in his step, where he began the elaborate routine of making his usual after-yoga smoothie. As the blender roared, he silently assured himself that his rug would be okay. Surely, it wouldn't be completely ruined by Doug's blatant lack of concern.

"Do you guys want a snack?" he asked from behind the kitchen wall. "We don't have much, but maybe some chips?" He peered into the refrigerator, spotting a can of half-used salsa.

"Chips would be awesome!" Doug shouted as though the apartment was twice its size and he stood the risk of not being heard.

Jimmy threw the chips on a plate along with the remains of the weeks-old salsa with the most amount of care he could muster up and rested it on the coffee table.

"How are things coming?" he asked.

"We're getting there, little by little," Doug replied with a wide smile as he pounced on the chips.

Luke shot Jimmy a private look, apologizing with his silent expression for the inconvenience his friend's presence was surely causing. "Thanks, James," he said knowingly. "We'll be done in twenty minutes, tops."

"Oh, no problem," Jimmy replied, his voice an octave higher than usual. "Take your time. I'm going to catch up on some reading anyway."

Living together had been an easy transition. The move happened unceremoniously, despite the scar that still marked his hand, a reminder of the day they made the leap into the next phase of their relationship. At first, things felt, for the most part, the same. Nothing much had changed, except for a few minor differences. The inadequacy of his tiny closet was now far more evident thanks to the addition of Luke's shirts and pants, tightly squeezed into the small bit of available space that remained unoccupied by Jimmy's ever-growing collection of clothes. Drawers filled to the brim with socks and underwear, some familiar, some foreign, greeted him in the mornings. On his way to the bed, he most often had to leap over sneakers and shoes that had mysteriously scattered themselves around the room as if there existed no alternate resting place for the presumptuous footwear. Strands of Luke's wavy, brown hair could now be found scattered on his pillow or gathered up near the drain of the shower. The kitchen had also undergone some changes. Luke had a talent for leaving dirty dishes in the sink, half-used cans of flat Coke in the fridge, pots filled with leftover meat sauce sitting on the stovetop. Nothing much had changed. Nothing hugely significant at least. But the apartment felt it. So did Jimmy.

He retired to the bedroom, a book nestled under his arm. He winced at the sight of Luke's sneakers lying in the middle of the room, his baseball cap nearby at the edge of the bed, but contained his frustration as he placed them neatly under the console table against the wall and leapt into the warm, inviting sheets. Sure, he had asked Luke, time and time again, to keep his sneakers in the closet in the living room—a closet specifically designated to house footwear and jackets—but perhaps it was too large of a request to expect any sort of immediate implementation. At the very least, to put them away in a corner somewhere would be sufficient enough instead of thoughtlessly leaving them in the middle of the room for someone to trip over.

"You okay?" Luke whispered as he slipped inside the bedroom and shut the door behind him.

"Of course," Jimmy replied. "Why? You guys done already?"

"I'm sorry about Doug," Luke apologized as he approached the bed.

"What do you mean?" Jimmy asked.

"I know you don't like having him over," Luke said, still careful to whisper so as not to be overheard. "I would have warned you he was here, but I didn't want to text you while you were in deep meditation or something."

"You're entitled to have friends over. It's your house too."

"Please," Luke replied with a glare. "I know you don't like him."

"He's your best friend. Of course I like him."

"Stop," Luke commanded softly as he sat down.

"What?" Jimmy asked, feigning confusion.

"You don't have to like all of my friends, you know. I don't like all of yours."

"Oh, really? And who is it that bothers you?"

"I'm not going there," Luke retreated as he looked away. His gaze landed on his sneakers nestled under the console table. "Sorry. Did I leave my sneakers lying around again?"

"You did," Jimmy replied.

"Really? Strange."

"Strange?" Jimmy asked. "They're always all over the place."

"Oh, please," Luke fired back dismissively.

Jimmy had not planned on starting a fight. Harping on Luke's disinterest in cleanliness made him feel like a nagging housewife. He loathed having to take on the role of frigid caretaker whose rules and regulations seemed to fall on deaf ears. He had, in fact, no intention of even bringing it up, but Luke's tone was already argumentative.

"Look. It's no big deal. I'm just saying, you could at least put them aside so I don't trip over them."

"It's no big deal? Well then why bring it up?" Luke asked, his voice rising.

"I didn't bring it up! You did."

"Why did you have to move them in the first place? What's the big deal if they're lying around? What—are you expecting visitors in the bedroom anytime soon?"

"It's not about that. It's just that I ask you time and time again to leave them in the closet and you never listen."

"I'm sorry I'm not actively thinking about where my shoes should go when I take them off, but who the fuck cares?"

"I do!"

Their voices had escalated well beyond whispers. Luke looked back at the closed door. "I can't do this right now." He leapt up from the bed in one sudden motion. A waft of anger hit Jimmy. "I'm sorry I left them lying around. Let me just finish this up with Doug and get him out of here."

"I never asked you to rush him out of here," Jimmy explained in a loud whisper. "Take your time."

Jimmy was relieved to be alone again when the door slammed shut. He cracked open the book with a heavy sigh. The bedroom's closed door only muffled Doug's obnoxiously loud indoor voice to a distant holler. Jimmy tried his best to block out the incessant chatter of Doug and his own troubled mind, but he failed to absorb the words on the page. Finally, he accepted defeat and surrendered to drowsiness as his head sank deep into the pillow.

He woke to Luke plopping down on the bed near him.

"The book's that interesting, huh?"

Jimmy rubbed sleep from his eyes as he propped himself up, resting his back on the bedhead. "How long was I asleep? You guys finished?"

"We're done," Luke replied with a smile. "For now at least. Doug's gone." An uncomfortable pause filled the air, waiting for someone to fill it. "Look, I'm sorry," Luke apologized.

"There's no need to be."

"Come on," Luke replied in disbelief.

"Everything's fine. Really." Sleep still weighed heavy on Jimmy as he sat up. He didn't have the energy to get into it, nor did he want to. It was a useless argument, too trite to warrant the fatigue.

"Get pissed at me. Scream at me. Throw my fucking sneakers in my face if you feel like it."

"Don't tempt me."

"Want me to go get them?" Luke asked with a grin. "I put them away. In the closet."

Jimmy peered past him. The space beneath the console table was empty. "Wow. I'm impressed."

"See. Not a total lost cause. Look, I know you like things a certain way and I know you're far more neat and orderly than I am, but sometimes it's too much for me to keep up with. And I don't want to have to always think and worry about these things."

"And I don't want to have to constantly nag about them either," Jimmy replied as his senses returned. "But I also don't want to have to jump over your shoes every time I enter the room."

"I don't *always* leave them in the middle of the room."

"No, you're right. You don't. Sometimes you leave them in the hallway, or in the kitchen, or on the rug in the living room."

"Now you're just being a jerk." Luke turned and fell into the bed, resting his head on the pillow near Jimmy's waist as he stared quietly at the ceiling.

"I don't know why we're arguing about your sneakers. It really didn't bother me, but you came in here ready to pick a fight for some reason."

"I wasn't trying to pick a fight, but I could tell you were pissed from the moment you got home."

"I wasn't pissed."

Luke turned his gaze to face Jimmy.

"I wasn't," Jimmy repeated.

"Come on. As soon as you saw Doug in here, you ran to the room."

"I had to take a shower!"

Luke stared blankly.

"All right. Maybe I was a bit disappointed to see he was still here, but that's only because—"

"Because you don't like him."

"I never said that."

"Trust me, it's obvious. I'm pretty sure he knows you don't like him."

"Really? You think? Don't make me feel like an asshole."

"Well, if the sneaker fits." Luke grinned like a cunning child used to getting his way. His unkempt hair rested wildly on his forehead, reaching for his eyebrows.

"Shut up." Jimmy reached over and brushed the hair away from Luke's face. He grabbed at a few strands of the wavy locks and twirled them between his fingers. The curls, when stretched out, grew to twice their original length. "Your hair's getting long."

"I know. I need a haircut."

"No. Don't cut it just yet. I like it like this." Jimmy gathered the mass of shaggy strands and pulled it back tightly. "A little bit more and you could rock one of those man buns."

"Never."

"Why not?" Jimmy asked. "I think you could actually pull it off."

"No. I can't."

"You underestimate yourself, my friend. You would rock the shit out of it."

"Really?" Luke asked. "You think?"

Luke climbed on top of Jimmy, working his body into the space between Jimmy's legs. Jimmy slithered down the bed, resting his head flat against the pillow as Luke's lips met his, pecking at them and pulling away.

Tiny, prickly bits of scruff covered Luke's jawline, creating a sandpaper-like texture that grazed against Jimmy's stubble. There was something appealing about the roughness of it. Luke's whole look had become more ragged, less delicate, creating an air of maturity that staggered Jimmy's senses into submission. Luke was more attractive than he had ever been before, and he seemed to know it. Jimmy pulled him closer, kissing his stubble-framed lips and tasting his moist, slithering tongue. His excitement grew, his body readying itself to go further when Luke slowed down. His tongue retracted. He pecked lightly at Jimmy's lips, one slow kiss after another as his eyes shut and his head fell to rest on Jimmy's shoulder.

Jimmy sighed. "Really?"

"I'm tired," Luke mumbled. "Let's take a nap," he said, cozying up further.

Jimmy shook his head. "I just woke up from a nap," he replied, but Luke was already dozing off. Jimmy peered down at the exhausted man on top of him, so quickly rendered lifeless. He looked toward the window. The sky's reflected light spread its usual golden hue across the room as it so often did as evening set in. Bits of purple and orange shone through, shades so radiant they almost seemed manufactured. Jimmy tried to wiggle himself free from his captor, but Luke weighed heavy on his chest. His breathing grew louder as he drifted away, content to ignore Jimmy's attempt to escape. "Come on—I have stuff to do," Jimmy whispered, shaking Luke lightly. Luke grunted. Jimmy sighed, already giving up.

Just as he began to shut his eyes he heard his phone ringing in the distance. He leaped into action, tossing Luke to the side as he jumped out of bed. The sound of his phone buzzing more and more violently led him out of the bedroom as Luke shouted angrily in his direction. "Sorry!" Jimmy shouted back as he answered Michael's call.

Chapter Fourteen

A DELICATE BREEZE washed over Jimmy. The soft wave of coolness grazed across his skin as he nestled farther into the blanket draped over his legs and arms. A thin layer of clouds covered the moon. Its filtered blue glow provided a dim ambient light to the rooftop terrace. They sat on mismatched beach chairs, old and haggard from neglect—muted, sun-damaged shades of blue and green, yellow and pink, the steel frames tarnished by rust and dents.

"You cold, babe?" Luke asked. "Wanna go inside?"

"No," Jimmy replied. "I'm okay."

"How could you be cold on this gorgeous night?" asked Alex with his arms stretched out, a joint in hand, his head aimed toward the glowing night sky. "We're in the middle of a beautiful transition—spring turning into summer. It's amazing," Alex proclaimed, sealing his eyes as he absorbed the night's air.

Of Luke's friends, Alex was the only one with whom Jimmy actually enjoyed spending time. There were others he didn't mind, some he tolerated, but Alex was always good company. He was, for the most part, a quiet man, but when he did speak it was with a thoughtful sincerity that Jimmy admired. Alex's tender insight and compassion was a welcome change of pace from Doug's often overbearing personality.

"About time," Luke added as he took the joint from Alex. "I'm sick of these never-ending winters. I'm this close to moving out of this fucking city."

"Oh really? And where exactly would you go?" Jimmy asked.

"Miami."

Alex chuckled. "You know, I could actually see that," he said.

Jimmy grimaced. "I wouldn't know what to do with all that sun."

"Really?" Luke asked. "I'd love it. Flip-flops and shorts every day."

"I think I'd be bothered by the same thing all year-round," Alex countered. "I need seasons. It feels unnatural otherwise."

Jimmy agreed. "It's like ninety degrees all the time over there. Even on Christmas!"

"Perfect!" Luke exclaimed. "No big-ass jackets and gloves to worry about."

"No way," Jimmy retorted. "The holidays are too magical in the city to give it up for hurricanes and excessive tanning."

Luke took hold of Jimmy's dangling hand as he whispered in a voice that played far quieter in his head than it did to those around him, "Let's spend Christmas together."

Jimmy smirked. "Isn't it a little early to be making plans for the holidays?" he asked.

"No, I'm serious. I want to spend it with you."

Luke's lazy eyelids remained only halfway opened, his grin even more asymmetrical than usual. Jimmy smiled at him adoringly.

"What did you guys do last year?" Alex asked.

"We spent it separately, with our families," Jimmy answered.

It was too soon to have spent the holidays together, or so Jimmy had decided. He'd thought it wisest to thwart any pressure over the matter by clarifying, as early as before Thanksgiving, that he would be spending the holiday with his family in Long Island. Secretly, he had hoped they could spend it together, but he'd decided it best to play it safe, certain that suggesting it would be going too far, worried that he might scare Luke away or make him feel obligated to agree.

"I thought about spending it together," Luke admitted. "But I didn't say anything,"

"Really?" Jimmy asked.

"I know how close you are with your family, and I didn't want to get in the way of that," Luke answered. "Plus, it was early on. I didn't know if it was okay to bring it up. Seems kinda stupid now, to be worried about how it seemed," he added with a quiet chuckle.

Jimmy stared at his Luke. He would have been elated a few months ago to know that the same thought had been running through their minds. The two had privately harbored the same hope but were both too scared, or nervous, or neurotic to bring it up. Only a few months had passed since the holidays, but it felt like another lifetime, when Jimmy had to tread lightly, holding back the confused mix of emotions that threatened to overpower his rational frame of mind. The period had been marked with a latent fear, a dark cloud covering the most brilliant light. He'd reminded himself constantly during those early days that Luke was a passing gift that would never really be his to keep. He was, in his way, preparing himself for the relationship's ultimate demise, bracing himself for reality's harsh blow that would inevitably arrive as it always had before. But the blow never came. Instead they became tightly bound to one another, their lives merging without hesitation like fibers of the same fabric weaving together at an alarming rate. It was hard to remember that there was a time, so recent, when sharing Christmas was too significant of a thought to entertain.

"I spent most of that time missing you," Jimmy admitted.

"So let's be together this year," Luke suggested again.

"Of course."

They would likely spend the holiday in their shared apartment. Maybe buy a small tree and decorate it together. Even hang stockings on the wall. Christmas night would probably be spent in Long Island, having dinner with Jimmy's family. Luke surely wouldn't mind having an excuse to be away from his quiet mother and father. He would likely share a drink with Harvey and laugh again at how foolish Jimmy was as a child. They would gather in the living room, sheltered from the winter's chill, chatting and laughing between moments of comfortable silence.

"There really is something about Christmas," Alex added. "It's like no other time."

"It is, after all, the most wonderful time of the year," Jimmy responded.

Alex laughed, prompting a cough that lasted close to a minute. "Yes. That it is," he muttered.

Jimmy freed his hand from Luke and took the joint, continuing the chain of succession that seemed to slow with each progressive round. He pulled in a drag, careful to only inhale a small amount, aware that his ever-loosening mind was getting away from him.

"I used to live for our family trips into the city during the holidays," Jimmy mentioned. "We'd visit the tree and

Bryant Park and FAO Schwartz. It was so magical as a kid. There was just something in the air. The whole city seemed to come to life with this burst of energy, like this final surge of excitement before hibernation." Jimmy stumbled through his words as he described the magic of Christmas, struggling to explain the inexplicable while in the midst of a pot-induced haze. When Luke countered, offering his disdain for the madness that was the holiday rush, Jimmy described that calming stillness that lay behind the shrilling chaos of the city. A stillness unique to that time of year, when bells chime and lights twinkle.

"It does instill a kind of sacredness into everything," Alex added. "Even Santa has become sacred in a way."

"Exactly!" Jimmy exclaimed, happy to find he still had an audience.

"Sacred?" Luke responded. "I think that may be a bit of an exaggeration."

"Not at all," Jimmy replied. "He's right up there with Jesus."

Alex laughed. A cloud of smoke burst out of his lungs. "Jesus may be the reason for the season, but Santa really is stealing the show."

Jimmy straightened his back as he sat upright. "Think about it," he began. "It's this wonderful fairy tale that we tell kids, and everyone willingly encourages it. No one wants to burst that bubble for a child. We all play along in reverence of his magic. It's sacred. Godlike even."

"I guess. But don't you think there's something wrong with that?" Luke asked. "Is it really a good idea to delude kids that way?"

"It gives kids something to believe in," Jimmy replied.

"Did you ever believe in Santa?" Alex asked Luke.

"Of course I did," Luke replied. "I don't remember it exactly, but I know I left out cookies and shit. But I do remember figuring it all out, and then feeling cheated like my parents had betrayed me in this horrible way. It was all a giant lie."

"See! You were hurt," Jimmy exclaimed. "What is important is not how crushed you felt afterward but how beautiful it was when you believed. Your level of disappointment is only proof of how intensely you believed. There's something really beautiful about that. There's something in that, I think, that's worth holding on to."

Luke appeared confused. His face grew tense. "Okay, but if you could prevent having to face that sort of disappointment, why wouldn't you? I'm not saying I wouldn't want my kid to believe in Santa. I'm just saying it presents this bigger issue. Really, isn't it basically the same as religion?"

"I guess, in a way," Jimmy replied.

"So are you making an argument for religion?" Luke asked sharply.

Jimmy hesitated for a moment, allowing the thought to penetrate. "Maybe. And why not? I think, at its core, religion can be a beautiful thing."

"It can also start wars!" Luke exclaimed

"Such is the power of belief," Alex added.

"Exactly," Jimmy agreed. "Whether for good or bad, you cannot deny there is power in belief."

"But blind belief in a lie is ridiculous!"

Luke's voice rose, getting louder the way it did during an argument. He was determined to prove his point. There was an air of superiority to that tone that irked Jimmy. Luke's strong-headed conviction had a way of blocking any contrary thought from bearing weight in a discussion. His mind, when made up, was impossible to budge.

"It is only a lie to the nonbeliever," Jimmy added carefully.

"But Santa doesn't exist!" Luke shouted.

"Of course not," Jimmy replied, out of breath as he struggled to contain his frustration. "I think we can all agree on that. The point is not Santa or religion or even God. It is belief itself that I think is most significant."

"I completely disagree! How can you say that?" Luke asked. "*What* you believe in is absolutely significant. It can't just be completely overlooked! What about religious fundamentalists killing people for what they believe in? Is that admirable?"

"Of course there is a dark side to belief, but I don't think we can fully blame the belief system itself so much as the believer," Jimmy attempted to explain. "People should never lose the ability to think for themselves or doubt and question things. All I'm saying is that in addition to a sense of rationale, believing in love or God or religion can add a certain beauty to life. Imagine how bleak our lives would be if we only ever lived with our minds."

Luke remained quiet for a moment, looking confused and frustrated, seemingly unable to find the words needed to build on his defense. Eventually his certainty boiled over. "You're not even religious!" he barked. "When was the last time you went to church?"

"What does going to church have to do with anything?" Jimmy asked, stunned and offended. "Just because I don't adhere to some set of dogmatic rules doesn't mean I don't believe in something bigger."

"Right, but you're sitting here arguing that religion is a good thing—"

"I said *belief* is a good thing," Jimmy interrupted. "You started us off on the whole religion conversation. Besides, I don't see how you can't see the potential it has for good. Nothing is black and white."

"Religion is just a way for stupid people to feel better about their utter insignificance," Luke retorted as his face turned red. "People needed answers to questions, so they made some shit up. How is believing in that a good thing?"

Silence filled the terrace, a burst of uncomfortable stillness. Luke shrugged, shaking off the discussion with a forced grin as he geared his attention forward. Jimmy sighed, unwilling to compete further. He surrendered to the flimsy, battered chair, resting his head against its cold, metal back as he stared into the cloudy night's sky, remembering a particular time as a child when he had gone to church with his aunt. She went every Sunday. Jimmy's mother rarely attended, but for some reason she had insisted Jimmy join his cousins.

The morning service had already finished by the time they arrived. The church had been nearly empty. Jimmy's aunt had seemed more contemplative than usual, quiet and distant. She sought refuge in her faith that day, the way she must have throughout her life. She sat with her hands clasped, eyes sealed, tears streaming down her face as she whispered. Jimmy's cousins were busy harassing each other with leaflets, shouting offenses to one another, but Jimmy's attention remained fixed on his aunt and her glowing expression of sincerity. It pulled him in, muting the sights and sounds around him. He felt for her, and with her. What had prompted the outpouring of emotions hardly mattered, all that did was the sincerity of her conviction. Though he couldn't quite understand it at the time, he was aware that what he'd witnessed was something significant, a feeling that would stay with him long after he left the church.

Luke shifted around uncomfortably on the metal chair as if searching for words to end the silence. Jimmy's gaze remained fixed on the empty sky above, but it was the image of his aunt that shone in his mind—love, pain, belief radiating out of her.

Chapter Fifteen

THE SINGER'S HAUNTING voice rose and fell through the air filling the converted warehouse with an eerie sense of mystery. She wore a long pink dress that dripped down her slender frame, its end billowing to the floor creating a puddle of pink silk at her concealed feet. She sang with her eyes closed, her arms spread out from her sides like wings with a mind of their own, gliding through the air without a destination. The chatter surrounding her didn't seem to faze her. The hordes of unappreciative passersby could not awake her from her gentle trance. She was lost in her own world of indecipherable lyrics and melody. Soaring high above. Jimmy was inexplicably drawn to her tranquility. The chatter around him also faded. The groups of people passing back and forth disappeared. The warehouse was empty but for him and her. No Blake, no Luke. Just Jimmy and the nightingale in the pink dress.

"They really filled it up this time." Luke approached with clear plastic cups filled nearly to the brim with red wine.

Jimmy took the offering and sipped its contents down to a less precarious level, but his attention remained fixed on the singer and the small group of musicians around her. A large man with hefty hands strummed a tiny mandolin. An intense woman, likely in her midforties, glided her bow back and forth along the strings of her cello. Jimmy tried to rekindle his moment of peace, but the distractions came flooding in.

The crowd's chatter intensified.

Inconsiderate strangers blocked his view.

Luke.

Luke's shirt was badly wrinkled, its puffy ends haphazardly tucked into his pants, billowing up like a parachute around his waist. Jimmy wanted to stay mad, to punish him for ruining the night. But how could he? His adorably unbothered Luke.

"You having an okay time?" Jimmy asked.

Luke nodded as he took a sip from the overfilled cup teeming with deep red liquid. "There's actually some cool stuff here."

"And a lot of shit."

Luke smiled. "Okay. Glad you said it and not me."

Almost every square inch of available wall space was occupied, quantity ruling over quality. The exhibit was a hodgepodge of art with no coherent concept, theme, style, or intent. A mix of mediums and tastes. Some pieces displayed a believable level of skill, while many others seemed to be first attempts, only slightly more elevated than a child's finger painting. Blake's work seemed to fall somewhere in the middle. He was clearly still discovering, but it was obvious that his paintings were more than just a hobby. With enough exploration it seemed he might realize his voice. Jimmy was thrilled to have received the invitation. It was inspiring to see his friend embrace a brave new passion. He was eager to show his support.

"Did you see Blake's pieces?" He asked.

"They were kinda hard to miss," Luke replied.

"They certainly stand out."

"That's putting it lightly."

The towering forty-eight-inch penis, oil on wood panel, was appropriately entitled *Precum,* referring, of course, to the faint stream of clear liquid leaking from the shaft. The painting was placed strategically at the end of a long hallway. The arresting image seemed to draw the crowd farther in as onlookers pointed and smirked, remarked and examined. It was, if nothing else, a conversation starter. Scattered around the giant cock were other startling images from the mind of Jimmy's immodest friend—abstract scenes of anal penetration, flagellation, and self-pleasure.

"We can take off if you want," Jimmy offered. His mood had cooled, but he had little energy left to enjoy the night as he had originally planned. Luke had drained it from him with his persistent one-sidedness and lack of interest.

"No, I'm fine," Luke replied. "No rush."

It had been a perfectly peaceful day before the argument. Jimmy's workload at the office had been light, and he'd made arrangements with Michael to leave at a normal hour so as not to be late. There was a spring in his step as he leapt through the elevator's steel doors and out the lobby. It was a rarity to leave the sometimes-suffocating confines of the office while the sun was still out. It was in its waning hours, burning with that final glow before being covered by shadow. It would most likely be dark by the time he emerged from the cavernous transit line on the other side of his commute. He made his way slowly to the train station, absorbing as much of the daylight as he could, though his eagerness to start his night out on the town urged him to hustle. It had been some time since he had seen Blake and Charlie. It seemed unfathomable that weeks, let alone months, could pass without getting together, but life had taken them on different roads. That night, however, he was determined to rekindle at least a small fragment of his previous life. Sadly, Luke was not as eager.

"I don't understand why you need me there," he said dismissively. "Why don't you just go on your own? You'd have more fun that way anyway."

Jimmy's enthusiasm evaporated as his clenched jaw struggled to hold back boiling anger. "I don't *need* you there. I want you there. Besides, you've known about this all week. It's not like I just sprang it on you. And you're not doing anything anyway."

"I just got home."

"So did I!"

"They're your friends. Why do I have to go? They don't even like me."

Jimmy sat down, taking a deep breath before attempting to express the importance the night bore. He described to Luke how he missed Charlie and worried he had turned his back on the life he had built for himself. He spoke honestly about the tiny achievements he had made back when he was alone. He struggled to explain how they resonated with a certain significance that he could never truly abandon. His words sprang from that place of deep-seated truth. It was more than just an art show. It was more than just Charlie or Blake. By the end of his monologue, Jimmy felt certain the disagreement would be laid to rest. Surely, the man he loved could, if not fully understand, at the very least appreciate his sentiment. But his reasoning seemed only to worsen the argument.

"Are you saying you're bored with me?" Luke asked, wide-eyed and infuriated.

Jimmy gasped. "I never said that."

"It's what you're implying by saying things were so great before me."

"You're not listening," Jimmy replied, his resolve extinguished. "Forget it. I'll go on my own."

Jimmy lifelessly made his way to the bedroom, accepting defeat as best he could. He began to close the door, but stopped himself from shutting it completely. He removed his shirt and replaced it with the one he had picked out early that morning while the sound of creaking floorboards drifted to his ear, Luke's unseen bustling echoing through the apartment with intent. It was replaced by the clanging of dishes in the sink followed by the sound of water running.

"Sorry I don't want to spend my night at some bourgie fucking art show pretending I give a shit," Luke murmured to himself, raising his voice just enough to be heard over the clatter he was creating in the kitchen. "It's not like I'm stopping you from going. Do what you want, but don't act like I'm somehow stifling you."

Jimmy sat at the edge of the bed and changed his shoes, trying hard to block the muffled rambling from penetrating his thoughts. It continued incessantly, Luke's private argument with himself, growing quieter until reaching an inaudible whisper. Eventually the water stopped running, and the room grew silent for a moment until the creaking of the apartment's wooden floors returned.

The tiny sliver of light emanating from the partly closed door grew in size as Luke emerged. He entered, walked to the bed, and took a seat at its end.

Jimmy rose.

"Are you not going to talk to me?" Luke asked sharply.

"I *was* talking to you. You weren't listening. But don't worry about it. It's fine. I'm going on my own."

Luke sighed, twisting and turning on the bed as Jimmy fastened his belt buckle. "Fine," he exhaled. "I'll go."

"Honestly, don't worry about it. I'm all set. Don't wait up."

"Will you wait a second?"

Jimmy turned around to face him.

"I said I'm going," Luke repeated.

"You don't want to. That's fine. I get it."

Luke stared silently at Jimmy's blank expression for a moment before getting up. "I'm going," he repeated, this time more sternly as he passed Jimmy on his way to the crammed closet. He sifted through the row of shirts that had worked its way to the deep recesses of the tight storage space, settling finally for a shirt that lay wrinkled on the floor near the hamper.

"WELL, LOOK WHO it is," Blake said as he approached, kissing Jimmy on the cheek. "I can't believe you actually showed up." He raised his glass to Luke. "Good to see you guys."

"Congratulations," Luke said as he raised his glass in return. "This is quite the impressive shindig. Your stuff really stands out."

"It's really great, Blake," Jimmy added. "I'm so happy for you."

"Thanks. But from the looks of it, they accepted work from anyone who submitted."

Jimmy and Blake caught up, filling each other in on the details of their everyday. Jimmy spoke of his promotion at work and his busy schedule. Blake mentioned Charlie and his boyfriend, in no subtle way hinting at a certain amount of discord in the relationship.

"Where is he?" Jimmy asked. "I was searching for him when I got here but he's nowhere around and he's not answering my texts."

"Probably fighting with his boyfriend somewhere. Actually, I wouldn't be surprised if he left already," Blake said, rolling his eyes.

Jimmy smiled to mask his disappointment. He glanced at Luke, silently blaming him for getting there late. Luke's free hand was pressed in his pocket as his eyes darted around in search of something that might interest him more than his present company.

"I am happy to see so many people showed up," Blake continued. "I wasn't sure when I sent out the invites. I'm tempted to roam around and eavesdrop," he added, leaning in with a whisper. "Listen in on all the shit-talking that must be going on."

"I'm sure everyone is more than supportive," Jimmy replied. "If anything they're just jealous that your giant dicks are on display for so many to see."

Blake grinned, seemingly unconvinced. "Drink up, you guys," he said, glancing down at Luke's nearly empty glass. "The booze is free, might as well get something out of the night. Time to mingle," Blake said, his fingers dancing in the air as he disappeared into the crowd.

Jimmy swallowed a large sip of his wine.

"Everything okay?" Luke asked.

"Yep," Jimmy replied, wanting to describe to Luke the unsettled feeling that sat at the pit of his stomach, his hopes to rekindle some former life with his friends so quickly quashed. But he was certain it would fall on deaf ears. He was alone in his discomfort. "Let's go home."

"Already? Don't you want to mingle?" Luke asked with spirit fingers twinkling, intended to mock Blake.

"No, not really. I don't really know anyone here, and Charlie's not answering me."

"Well, let's wait a little," Luke suggested. "You wanted to see him. Maybe he'll show up. In the meantime, might as well take advantage of that bar."

Luke took Jimmy's hand and ushered him through the crowd to the small bar where he ordered cocktails, opting to step it up from the bitter red wine. His attitude had lightened, playfulness taking the place of tiredness as if in an effort to brighten Jimmy's mood. Jimmy appreciated the effort. It was, he supposed, Luke's way of apologizing. They drank quietly, finishing their drinks and ordering another round. "We came all this way, might as well," Luke said as he handed Jimmy another filled glass of whiskey and Coke.

The music grew louder. The elegant singer in pink had packed her things, replaced by a DJ wearing a vintage suede hat, the unnecessarily large brim covering most of his face. His T-shirt hung loosely over his slender body, almost reaching his knees, more so resembling a dress than a shirt. His headphones carelessly rested over one ear as he studied the screen of his laptop, preparing his next song, one that would no doubt sound indecipherably similar to the current stream of noise emanating from the oversized speakers.

The bar's proximity to the speakers rendered any attempt at conversation useless, but Jimmy was happy to be free of the need to talk. He, instead, enjoyed the surge of warmth that traveled more intensely through his body with each passing sip. Luke's shoulders began to sway, loose and out of rhythm. His head bobbed like a bird searching for worms the way it did whenever he danced.

"Is it just me, or does this no longer feel like an art show?" Jimmy shouted. A crowd had formed near the DJ as the warehouse art exhibit turned into a makeshift EDM party. Only a few irritated attendees still struggled to see the art as the open space turned into a dance floor, people loosely swaying, alcohol leaping from ever-emptying cups.

"Only in Brooklyn," Luke said with a grin. "It's the free booze. Everyone's wasted."

"I'm feeling pretty tipsy, myself," Jimmy shouted.

Luke chugged back the remainder of his drink and grabbed Jimmy's waste, encouraging him to dance. Jimmy smiled and bounced in place for a little while, but his head grew light and he struggled for balance. His bladder had hit max capacity.

"I have to pee," he shouted into Luke's ear.

"Me too!"

They slipped through the crowd to the back of the warehouse. A few people waited in the narrow hallway leading to the warehouse's one bathroom. Luke threw his back against the wall, leaning on it for support.

"I don't feel too good," he said. His face had a warm glow—that redness that appeared whenever he was angry, or aroused, or had too much to drink. He never did manage alcohol very well.

"One too many free cocktails," Jimmy replied. "I can't believe with all these people, there's only one bathroom."

Luke pried his back off the concrete wall, defiantly planting his feet on the ground as if to prove his vitality. He ran his hands across his face and exhaled into his palms, approaching Jimmy with an exaggerated smile. Jimmy smiled back, slightly amused.

"You look nice tonight," Luke noted. "Is that a new shirt?"

It was easier to be heard in the hallway. The noise around them faded into a dull grumble.

"Actually, it is," Jimmy replied, happy that Luke had finally noticed. Luke's face was now even redder, his hair slightly disheveled. His eyes weighed heavy. He looked like Luke, first thing in the morning. "You look nice too," Jimmy added. Luke-first-thing-in-the-morning was Jimmy's favorite. "Thanks for coming."

Luke shuffled closer, taking his place in line behind Jimmy as a woman exited the bathroom in a hurry. "Only one more," he whispered into Jimmy's ear. "We're next."

He wrapped his arms around Jimmy's waist and pulled him near as the man ahead of them moved forward. Luke pressed his chest against Jimmy's back as he breathed heavily. Warmth glided across Jimmy's neck. Luke smelt of liquor and sweat. The scent soared through Jimmy as the tiny strands of hair on his arm stood on end. He rested his hands on Luke's arms as they continued waiting in silence until they were finally left alone as the bathroom door opened and closed again. The narrow hallway was empty. Jimmy's eyelids fell as he surrendered his body toward Luke's.

"Finally some privacy," Luke whispered as his body began to sway, pushing Jimmy closer to the bathroom door. His hold traveled south to Jimmy's crotch where his hands gently massaged the area.

"Stop it," Jimmy whispered as his eyes closed again.

Luke kissed his neck, grazed Jimmy's ear with his tongue, pressed his pelvis farther into his back. Jimmy's heart began to quicken. His breath shortened. He could feel himself stiffening little by little.

"Hey. Really," he whispered. "Stop." His voice grew stern, but his sighs told a different story. Luke continued to press closer, his fast-growing bulge prodding Jimmy's back. "At least wait till we're inside." Jimmy peeled away, freeing himself from his seducer as the door swung open and the man exited. Luke grabbed a hold of Jimmy's waist again, and forcefully ushered Jimmy into the vacant bathroom. The door slammed shut behind them.

Luke spun Jimmy around, pinning him against the cold steel door as their lips crashed together. Their tongues whirled. Jimmy grabbed on to Luke's ass, pulling his body closer. Luke ran his hand up and down Jimmy's chest, gliding across his new shirt. He continued rubbing Jimmy's torso until making his way to Jimmy's crotch, where he forced his way into Jimmy's pants.

Jimmy moaned, swinging his head back against the door as Luke touched his throbbing flesh. Luke kissed his neck, pecking and nibbling. He removed his hand and reached for Jimmy's belt buckle. The clasp refused to budge.

"Just unzip it," Jimmy commanded, out of breath.

Luke dropped to his knees and unzipped Jimmy's pants. He reached past the thin flap in his boxers and released the firm mass of flesh. He was careful at first, as he began to stroke it, leaning back to examine his prey before pouncing.

Jimmy trembled as Luke's warm mouth received him.

Luke worked furiously up and down the shaft, swirling his tongue around the tip with an unprecedented hunger. His hands partook in the action, gliding across the drenched surface as his mouth worked more and more hastily. Jimmy grabbed a hold of Luke's disheveled hair and tugged at it. He could hear a small wince struggle to escape Luke's occupied mouth. The tiny plea for relief was exhilarating. Jimmy pulled harder, grabbing chunks of Luke's hair in his grasp as he pushed and pulled, commanding Luke back and forth with growing force. Jimmy moved faster, sliding in deeper and deeper until Luke gagged, on the verge of choking. Luke resisted, pushing back, pressing his hands against Jimmy's stomach as he pried himself away and gasped for air. Jimmy let go, allowing Luke time to catch his breath. Luke panted, his arms propped up against Jimmy. Finally, he exhaled as his breath returned to normalcy.

Once revitalized, Jimmy chucked Luke's hands off his stomach and grabbed his hair again, lining him up for another round. Luke's lips parted. Jimmy thrust forward. Luke's eyes peeled open as he allowed himself to be commanded. Jimmy shoved his cock deep into Luke's mouth, forcing Luke to devour him entirely. Luke's eyes watered, his whole body convulsing as if trying to exorcise a demon. A thick stream of saliva oozed from his mouth. His face turned stark red. Jimmy held him in place as tears streamed down Luke's cheeks. Finally, he released his hold. Luke pulled back, freeing his mouth as he swallowed hard, gasping for air. He took a moment, peering down at the pool of spit on the floor as he caught his breath. Before long, Luke reached for Jimmy's slippery cock. His hand ran across the surface, wet with mucus. Jimmy's eyes sealed shut as his arms dropped to his side. His head fell back against the door as he let Luke take over. Luke's hand continued where his mouth left off, persistently working up and down the shaft, squeezing with force, intent on finishing the job despite being battered and overworked. A surge of warm liquid came gushing out, shooting forward in spurts. Jimmy grabbed onto Luke's shoulders. He shuddered as his body drained, a prolonged, jilted burst of relief.

When the final drop had fallen, Luke released his grasp and sighed exhaustedly. His hands fell to his thighs as he sat on the floor, gathering his composure for a moment. He rose in silence, wiping his hands and mouth clean with the end of his wrinkled shirt. Jimmy caught his breath and zipped up, his eyes unable to make contact with Luke who stood motionless in front of him. They stood silent for a moment until Jimmy looked up, his eyes meeting the helpless, injured man in front of him. An agonizing knot fastened itself in the pit of Jimmy's stomach, guilt threatening to suffocate. Luke's eyes were bloodshot and watering. Jimmy reached over and flattened his boyfriend's shirt, tucking it into his pants, hoping to wipe clean his regret. Luke allowed Jimmy to redress him as his arms dangled at his sides.

Jimmy moved to the sink, an added dose of urgency motivating his step. He wet his hands and combed them through Luke's disheveled hair, slicking it back, defining the part, careful to put every strand in its place. He wiped remnants of tears and saliva from Luke's face, caressing his skin, working with concern and fear, covering up his shame like a child cleaning a spill.

"I'm good," Luke muttered beneath a sigh.

Jimmy stood silent for a moment watching him. Luke stared past Jimmy, eyes fixed on the door ahead. Jimmy kissed him and took his hand as they exited.

They walked silently out of the empty hallway and back into the mass of confusion.

"Let's get out of here," Jimmy shouted as he turned back to Luke. He held his hand tightly, squeezing it with all the compassion and guilt and confusion that was brewing inside, raising it to his chest so as to keep Luke close as they pushed and shoved through the crowd of people.

"Jimmy?" a voice hollered. It pierced through the air like an arrow headed straight for the bull's-eye.

"Chris?" Jimmy gasped as he turned to find the stranger from his past approaching. "What are you doing here?"

Jimmy released Luke's hand as Chris swooped in and hugged him, wrapping his arms around Jimmy tightly and lingering for a moment. His touch was uninvited, but familiar. There was, after all, a time when their bodies knew each other well, a time when Jimmy craved him. But that was another lifetime ago, and the memories that came rushing back of their heated, misguided, explosive affair made Jimmy cringe in disgust. He pulled his head back, eager to be released.

Luke stepped forward, offering his hand as the two parted. "I'm Luke," he asserted.

Chris shook Luke's hand, introducing himself as a friend of Jimmy's. "How have you been?" he asked Jimmy, with an affectionate smile.

"Good," Jimmy answered. "Really good, actually."

"Blake didn't mention you were here," Chris shouted as he leaned in close to Jimmy, struggling to be heard over the piercing noise still blasting from the surrounding speakers. Chris joked about the absurdity of the event, the out-of-place DJ, the boldness of Blake's art. Jimmy laughed uncomfortably, his feigned enthusiasm working hard to mask the sinking feeling of disgust that sucked the wind out of his lungs. Chris was quick to share details about what he had been up to—a new job, a new boyfriend, a recent trip to Peru; eager to brag about his exciting life as if to finally prove his worth to Jimmy who had once cast him aside. Jimmy nodded, only catching bits and pieces of the story as his eyes darted back and forth between Chris and Luke, wedged between pillars of regret and guilt.

Luke waited on the sidelines as Chris leaned close to Jimmy, whispering in his ear and lightly caressing his arm.

"So are you two together?" Chris asked.

"Yes. We are," Jimmy replied, finally able to get a word in.

Chris's eyes sharpened as he nodded in Luke's direction. Luke forced a smile. "I'm happy to see you're doing well," Chris added with a forced smile of his own. "So how long have you two been dating?"

Jimmy hesitated, surprised and offended by the sudden inquisition. He longed for the interaction to end, to hide in a corner somewhere, free of the pressure.

Luke answered, "It's been—what—a year now." He looked at Jimmy and took his hand.

"Not quite," Jimmy replied. "Almost, though."

"Wow, that's something," Chris replied. "Has it really been that long since I've seen you?"

"I guess so." Jimmy smiled uncomfortably. "You know, we were actually just leaving," he added. He turned to Luke, cueing their exit.

"How do you two know each other, exactly?" Luke asked, pretending to be oblivious of the details.

Jimmy stared at Luke for a moment. "We met through Charlie."

"Oh, of course," Luke replied with a fakeness Jimmy had never before seen on him. "I think you've mentioned him before."

Chris did his best to alleviate the obvious tension in the air, asking Luke what he thought about the art show, repeating a good deal of the mundane pleasantries he had exchanged with Jimmy in some ill-received effort to include Luke. Luke's responses were short and disinterested. Jimmy smiled and laughed in the wings, hoping to make up for Luke's rudeness and keep the conversation civil. Finally, when Chris had given up and a moment of silence presented itself, Jimmy jumped in with an excuse to flee.

The ride home was spent in silence. Jimmy stared blankly out the window, watching quiet Brooklyn streets zoom by, all the while wishing he could be alone for a moment to retreat from the confusion that filled him. When they arrived home Luke took his shoes off and placed them in the closet. Jimmy watched warily as Luke unbuttoned his shirt and made his way to the bedroom.

"Are you going to shower?" Jimmy asked.

"I'm beat," Luke replied. "I just want to sleep."

He stripped down to his boxers, jumped into bed, and pulled the covers over his bare skin. The room was silent and dark. Jimmy kicked off his shoes and undressed. He hesitated to join Luke. Perhaps, he thought, it would be better to sleep on the sofa. He did crave, after all, a minute alone, a chance to make sense of the mess. Eventually he crept into bed, careful to leave enough space between he and Luke. The discomfort in his stomach still lingered. He could feel it churning, demanding attention. He turned to his side to face Luke's back, waiting for a reaction. He longed to shake him, to scold him, to apologize.

"Hey. Are you okay?" Jimmy asked.

Luke responded with an exaggeratedly tired grunt.

"I'm sorry I made you come out tonight," Jimmy said. "I really wish I hadn't."

Luke sighed. His frustration bore through the air, its razor-sharp edge cutting with precision.

Jimmy waited for more. "Are you just going to ignore me?"

"I'm not ignoring you," Luke answered.

"Can we talk?"

"I'm tired."

Jimmy placed his hand on Luke's arm. "Come on. It's barely past eleven."

Luke sighed again, the blade duller this time around. He turned to rest on his back. "What do you want to talk about?" he asked with his gaze fixed to the ceiling.

"I'm sorry about tonight," Jimmy said as his hand moved to Luke's chest.

"There's nothing to be sorry about." Luke turned his head to face Jimmy.

"There is." Jimmy's eyes filled as he relived the aggression in the bathroom. His frustration had taken over, turning him into a person he'd barely recognized. It had been invigorating in the moment—taking what he wanted—

but the excitement had stemmed from a place of anger, even hatred. It wasn't who they were, and he cringed to imagine it was who they were becoming. "I'm sorry," he repeated as a tear trickled down his cheek.

Luke turned to lie on his shoulder, his body now geared toward Jimmy. "I'm not mad," he said. He leaned in and kissed Jimmy.

Jimmy smiled as he swallowed hard, holding back more tears from falling. His hand fell on Luke's face and glided across the scruffy surface. Tiny hairs scraped against his palm along the way. "When was the last time you shaved?" he asked.

"Almost two weeks."

Jimmy leaned in and kissed him, hopeful that they might return to some state of normalcy and forget the whole night entirely. They inched closer to each other as they opened their mouths. Luke ran his fingers through Jimmy's hair, tugging at it slightly as he bit his bottom lip. He pressed his face against Jimmy's, gliding cheek against cheek as he maneuvered himself on top of Jimmy. The grit of Luke's facial hair grazed across Jimmy's bare skin like sandpaper. It was bearable at first until it gained traction and began to tread with greater force. Luke continued more and more vehemently—his nose, forehead, cheeks rubbing against every contour of Jimmy's face like a dog burying its face in dirt. His sealed lips skated across Jimmy's back and forth.

"Stop," Jimmy struggled to utter. His face had turned red, sore from the sandpaper's unforgiving touch. Luke added pressure, pushing himself closer with more resolve, squashing Jimmy with his weight. "Stop!" Jimmy shouted. He twisted from side to side, struggling to free himself until finally managing to create a small gap by pressing his hands against Luke's chest.

Luke pushed back, pinning Jimmy down under his weight. He kissed and licked, nibbling on Jimmy's ear as Jimmy teetered between compliance and refusal like a confused captor, shifting himself as he struggled to break free. Luke bit Jimmy's neck and shoulder. He grabbed Jimmy's crotch. Jimmy winced in pain. Luke yanked harder. Jimmy cried out.

"What the fuck!" Jimmy shouted as he pushed his open palm into Luke's face. His arm extended fully, widening the gap. Luke shoved back. Jimmy maneuvered his legs out from under Luke's and used them to push him to the other side of the bed with one swift kick.

"What's your problem?" Luke shouted. "You just fucking kicked me!"

"I told you to stop! One minute you're too tired to talk, the next you're attacking me like a fucking dog."

Luke laughed devilishly. "You didn't seem to mind earlier."

Jimmy gasped as he sat up, resting his back on the bedhead. He was guilty. Perhaps he deserved to be manhandled. He wiped his face clean of Luke's sweat and saliva. "I'm sorry about what happened in the bathroom," he repeated. "I don't know what came over me."

Luke scoffed at Jimmy and worked his way under the sheets. "Forget it," he said, throwing the blanket over his shoulder. "It's not like I didn't like it."

Jimmy watched Luke's back twist and turn as he settled in, a wall erecting between them. Luke grumbled indistinctly under his breath. Jimmy sank back into the bed in defeat, a stranger in his own room. He turned his back to Luke, facing the other end of the room, unable to close his eyes.

"This is why I didn't want to go out in the first place," Luke grumbled.

Jimmy kept quiet. He had little energy left to apologize again.

"I don't like being around your friends," Luke continued. "They're all condescending bitches sitting on their make-believe fucking thrones all full of shit. And you're shitty when you're around them."

Jimmy breathed heavy.

"I honestly don't understand what you see in people like Blake," Luke added. "And *Chris*! Are you fucking kidding me?"

Jimmy longed to fight back, to lash out in some way, but he kept quiet.

"Sure he's hot," Luke continued, his tone growing nastier with each word. "But, come on. *That* guy? Really? I never would've thought you were so superficial."

"Now you're just being an asshole," Jimmy finally whispered.

"Of course. I'm always the asshole."

Silence sank into the room as the space between them grew. There was so much to say, so much to resolve, but Jimmy was at a loss with where to begin. He wanted to fire back—to criticize Luke for being so high and mighty, to insult Doug and Alex in return. He wanted to explain how alone he had been feeling for weeks, how confused he was about where he was heading and what the future held. Luke was the one person left who might understand, but lately every attempt at expression turned into something else, his words getting misconstrued to work against him.

"You're not an asshole," Jimmy replied. "But I wish you would talk to me honestly instead of just attacking me."

Luke thrust the covers off and sat up to face Jimmy. "And what exactly do you want me to say?" he asked. Jimmy rose, hesitantly gearing his attention to Luke. "That I'm tired of trying to be something I'm not!"

Jimmy squinted, studying Luke, hoping he might find some answers on his infuriated face, some explanation as to why Luke felt he had to be anyone other than who he was.

"I see the way you look at me," Luke continued. "The way your friends see me. I'm a mess, I have the body of a twenty-something-year-old dad, my shirts are too big. It's never good enough. What do you want from me? Should I start wearing ridiculous loafers and taking trips to Peru like that idiot ex of yours?"

"No! Of course not. Where is this coming from? You've got it all wrong."

Luke sprang up from the bed and grabbed his pillow. "Your friends make me feel like shit, and you make me feel like shit. I'm fucking over feeling like shit."

"How do I make you feel like shit?" Jimmy asked as Luke stormed out of the room.

The sofa creaked under the weight of Luke's body crashing down on it. Jimmy sat motionless, staring at the door as if Luke might change his mind and come running back. But he didn't. Moments passed as Jimmy sat frozen. His phone beeped. It was a text from Charlie asking where he had gone.

"We're going out for drinks," Charlie wrote. "Bring Luke."

Jimmy tossed the phone back onto the nightstand and sank into the bed.

Chapter Sixteen

THE SUMMER'S HEAT rose from the concrete pavement in waves, almost visibly—the air thick with humidity. Jimmy hid under the canopy, struggling to see past the crowd that had gathered near small monitors. Crewmembers hurdled over each other, fighting for space, all eyes on the screens as the director yelled, "Action!"

Being on set was a far less glamorous affair than Jimmy had imagined. It was mostly a bunch of people eating snacks and shouting at each other. Packaged cookies, bags of chips, and fresh fruit lined a plastic folding table. A jar filled with M&M's sat at the table's edge. Crewmembers came and went, stuffing their sweaty faces with the processed foods, mostly ignoring the fruit. Some hollered things into headsets with deluded notions of self-worth, wiping their dirty hands on cargo shorts that hung loosely off their waists, low enough to reveal the unsightliness of frumpy boxers and even the occasional butt crack. Having a walkie-talkie seemed to be reserved for the more important crewmembers, ones who wielded their useless powers with an inflated sense of authority.

The warehouse was massive and equipped with central air. Of course, Freestyle was shooting outside the building, using the warehouse's exterior wall covered by steel and brick as the model's backdrop. Her role was simple, one-dimensional, in many ways offensive, but she played it with class. She strutted along the wall in painfully high heels, discovered the glass at the end of her path, and, with an admirable amount of wonder and surprise, drank the mysteriously placed vodka with enough seduction and sex appeal to make even Jimmy take notice.

Michael sat on a chair near the director, his legs crossed, notepad in hand. He twirled his pen around his fingers as he squinted at the screen, his mouth clenched. Take after take, he continued to fiddle with his pen in silence. Jimmy watched in apprehension from a safe enough distance. It was only a matter of time until Michael exploded. The director worked in haste, arranging and rearranging the shot as Michael's silent disapproval continued to brew.

"Cut," the director hollered as he ran over to the wall and moved the glass an inch to the left, and then an inch to the right, and then an inch back to the left. "That's it." He scurried back to the canopy.

Michael's pen hovered over the clean pages of his notepad, his eyes fixed on the yellow paper as the director returned to his chair. "You know what," Michael began. The director turned to him, his breath caught in his throat. "Let's take a break for a second," Michael continued.

"Should we roll on this one first?" the director asked.

Michael shook his head and sprang up from his chair. The director followed as they made their way toward the model.

The crew stood frozen, all eyes watching Michael and the director move the green stool from one spot to another. The painted stool would be digitally removed by one of the artists back at the office. They would likely replace it with a computer-generated cloud or maybe a boulder of some sort. The sky above the wall would become an exaggerated dreamscape. Jimmy had examined the design boards with mocked-up images for weeks before the shoot, studying the projected end goal with doubt. Now that it was in the midst of being created, he was certain it was even less inspiring than he had originally imagined it would be.

After their discussion, Jimmy was assigned the task of "running back to the office" to pick up one of the 3D artists and bring them to set so that they could approve the new setup and make sure the updated placement wouldn't present any unforeseen problems down the road—as if journeying from Long Island City to Manhattan and back during the waning hours of this intensely hot afternoon was at all a minor undertaking. He nodded, silently cursing his boss for allowing the intern to take the day off. When Jimmy was halfway to the office he received a series of texts from Michael listing more errands that required immediate attention: picking up his laptop from the shop, making copies of the sketches he had left on his desk, even grabbing his jacket from the dry cleaners so that he could head straight home when they finally wrapped on set. Jimmy cringed at that last one, but a smiley face did follow it, along with "xoxo." He supposed, in some way, it made up for it.

By the time he returned with Mark and the other requested necessities, the sun was setting and the entire crew was in full panic mode. Crewmembers scurried from one end of the set to the next, arranging and rearranging lights and filters as they shouted at each other, emotions elevated. Jimmy returned to his spot at the end of the canopy, crossed his arms, and observed the chaos unfold around him. Mark, the chosen artist who instantly became man of the hour, pointed and directed as crewmembers obeyed, moving objects without question until finally he was satisfied and gave Michael the go-ahead. Two takes and one disgruntled director later and they were done.

"Let's get the hell out of here," Michael suggested as he approached Jimmy. "What do you say we get a drink?"

Jimmy agreed. "Wait, I thought you wanted to run home as soon as this was done," he added with an intentional degree of sass.

"Now I need a drink."

Jimmy didn't protest. He had been teetering between boredom and exhaustion all day and could also use a release.

Once they were seated at high-top tables, the sweat that clung to their skin mostly dry, Michael suggested Jimmy invite Luke. "I can't believe I've only ever met him once," he added. "We can fill him in on how exciting today was."

"So much excitement," Jimmy replied sarcastically. "I don't think he'd be up for coming out. He's usually pretty tired by the time he gets home from work."

Michael asked what life was like now that he and Luke were a couple living together. "Great," Jimmy replied overzealously. He described a scene not far from reality, only sweeter and without the many roadblocks. He did mention that it required a certain amount of adjusting to settle into sharing his life with someone, but he left out the specifics, choosing to keep private the silence that had befallen them. The arguments had stopped. He was, at least, grateful for that. But in its place Jimmy and Luke settled into a strange state of ignorance, both happily overlooking the problems that boiled beneath the surface.

"I'm glad you're happy," Michael said. "You deserve it."

Jimmy forced a smile as Michael chugged the remainder of his drink and ordered another round. Michael held his alcohol well. His speech stayed steady as they continued drinking; his attention grew more focused. It seemed, in fact, that the more he drank the more engaged he became.

"I've got to thank you," he said to Jimmy. "You were a real help today. But I know this spot is crap and I know you know it."

Jimmy flinched ever so slightly as he looked for a way to justify his obvious disinterest in the shoot, but eventually he surrendered to Michael's claim, shrugging with a smile. Michael laughed. His hand fell on Jimmy's. He squeezed it. "I knew it!" he proclaimed. "You hate it!"

"It's not that I hate it," Jimmy began.

"You hate it!" Michael interrupted. His hand remained on top of Jimmy's, though his grip loosened as he shook his head, a devious smile plastered on his face. "You're not wrong. It is crap. I'm no idiot. I hate it too—but it's what they want." His expression softened.

Jimmy peered down, examining the scene on the tabletop, searching for a way to free his hand without offending. When he glanced up, Michael was staring. His expression was blank, but his eyes spoke volumes. He waited in silence as if expecting Jimmy to provide some sort of signal that it was safe to go further. Jimmy grinned uncomfortably.

"I really appreciate having you around, James. You're a real asset to the team." Michael began to glide his fingers across the back of Jimmy's hand, drawing invisible circles on his flesh.

"I'm just happy to be a part of it all," Jimmy replied, his breath shortening, the space around him closing in. "Maybe we should get going," he suggested. "It's getting late."

"So soon?" Michael asked. Finally, he released his hold. Jimmy caught his breath, certain that the moment had passed, but Michael inched closer, slithering toward Jimmy, a man on a mission. "Let's go somewhere else, get another drink."

For a fleeting moment, the offer sounded enticing. The space between them vanished. But then, Jimmy cringed. This wasn't the Michael he had imagined himself with years ago. This, surely, was not the same man he had admired, looked up to, hoped to emulate one day. That Michael would never make such a thinly veiled pass. That Michael knew Jimmy better than to think he might be up for a one-night affair; that he could ever possibly cheat on Luke.

"I really should get going," Jimmy said as he rose.

"Okay, fine." Michael retreated. "You're right. It's late." He rose, poised and confidently unaffected. "Besides, we have work tomorrow." When they stepped outside, Michael was notably more boisterous, joking about the shoot and the director's phony accent. "We'll do what we can with it. It'll still be worth something in the end," he asserted, slipping back into work-mode as if nothing had happened.

Jimmy smiled agreeably. "See you in the morning," he added as Michael vanished. Disgust sank into Jimmy's pores as he scurried toward the train station. He longed to rush home, jump in the shower, and rinse his skin of it along with the dried sweat that sat like glue on his body. Maybe once cleaned up, he could forget that cunning, blank stare, so brashly confident. Luke would surely help. One touch, or hug, or kiss and the night could be wiped clean. Hopefully he wasn't already asleep.

Chapter Seventeen

THE LUNCH RUSH was in full swing. Jimmy had been waiting patiently for twenty minutes before his name was finally called. He entered the loud, crowded café and was escorted to a table in the far-off corner.

"Just one?" the bubbly hostess asked as she flashed her brilliant white smile in Jimmy's direction.

"Two, actually. He's on his way."

"No problem. Did you put your order in already?" she asked.

"I did," Jimmy replied, handing her the plastic badge with his number.

Taking time out of work to meet for lunch was unusual, but not unprecedented. Jimmy remembered a similar rendezvous not so long ago as he waited alone at the table. It was early on in their relationship, when the air was filled with excitement and the world around them hardly existed. They had been texting all day while both at work. Playful banter eventually slipped into more promiscuous terrain. They joked about the things they might do with each other if they had the chance, inventing scandalous scenarios— risqué and thrilling encounters filled with heat and passion. Eventually, they settled on meeting for lunch. Jimmy had waited anxiously in a café not unlike this one. Luke had arrived with a sinister grin glued to his face. He approached but did not sit. He leaned in and took Jimmy's hand.

"Where are we going? Are we not eating?" Jimmy asked as he rose, bewildered but giddy.

"Just come with me," Luke commanded.

He escorted Jimmy across Gramercy Park to a small run-down hotel. The dimly lit lobby was sparsely filled with furniture from the early nineties. Jimmy anxiously took a seat on a plush crème-colored couch, sinking into the thin layer of dust that covered its surface while Luke made arrangements at the front desk. Jimmy played with his watch, rotating it around his wrist back and forth to divert his mind from over assessing the mix of nerves and excitement that brewed within. They had jokingly mentioned skipping out of work and getting a hotel room, but he never imagined they would follow through. Luke's hand fell warmly on his shoulder.

"Let's go."

They rode up to the fourth floor in silence. The hallway was covered in shades of pink and turquoise. Prints of Western landscapes lined the walls—their pale, faded tones matching the shade of the dated wallpaper. It took some amount of manipulation and brute force to open the room door. Luke laughed when it finally swung forward.

"Sorry," he apologized as they entered. "Not exactly the Waldorf."

The room matched the building's overall aesthetic, its lack of concern for modern standards of design and cleanliness in perfect harmony with the drab lobby and halls. The carpet was a deep shade of maroon, darker stains dispersed throughout like markers of its history.

"It's okay," Jimmy said. "It'll do." They were both selective with their words, more reserved and quiet than usual, silenced by the peculiarity of the afternoon.

Jimmy locked the door behind him while Luke walked to the back of the small room and pulled the patterned drapes closed. A cloud of dust filled the air as the fabric slid across the curtain rod hiding their actions from the onlooking world.

Jimmy's hands shook as he stood near the bed, tentatively hovering over it, uncertain of how to proceed. The sheets were a brilliant shade of white, a stark contrast to the surrounding clash of dated colors and prints, and a welcome bit of cleanliness in an otherwise uninviting room.

Luke approached, almost dancing his way to Jimmy. Once stationed in front, he reached over and began to unfasten each button of Jimmy's shirt. Jimmy stared at Luke as he worked, studying his glistening lips and dominant brow, his excitement growing with each freed button. Luke parted the two halves of the shirt, exposing Jimmy's bare chest. He paused for a moment, taking it in before touching. He gently caressed Jimmy's skin, gliding his hand up and down his torso. Jimmy's heart pounded as warmth traveled across his flesh. Luke inched forward. Jimmy parted his lips. His eyes rolled back as he slipped his tongue into Luke's mouth. He grabbed Luke tightly, feeling the hard protrusion of his rib cage through his shirt. He tugged at Luke's polo and peeled it off. Luke charged forward, this time pressing Jimmy up against the wall. Their bare chests smashed together. Jimmy ran his hands up and down Luke's bare back as he breathed him in.

"I want you to fuck me," Luke whispered, already out of breath.

Jimmy smiled as he reached down into Luke's pants and grabbed his bare ass. "Gladly."

JIMMY COULD SMELL the room again as he sat waiting in the crowded café. That heavy scent of sweat and sex. He had devoured every part of Luke, appeasing an appetite that seemed to reach its peak that thrilling afternoon. He pushed and pulled, clawed at flesh and tugged at hair. Afterward, they rested, embracing each other before continuing again, drunk on the desire to consume one another in every way possible.

"The quinoa salad?" a waiter asked as he approached with a large plate almost brimming over. Moments later, Luke arrived, scurrying to the back table after spotting Jimmy.

"You been waiting long?" he asked. "Sorry, I decided to take a cab—bad idea."

"It's okay. I went ahead and ordered for you."

Jimmy worried, at first, about Luke's reason for wanting to meet so suddenly. Luke's voice had been frantic on the phone. It was either good news or bad news, but judging from Luke's now obvious gleefulness, it was likely the former.

"So what's going on? Everything okay?" Jimmy asked.

Luke smiled brightly, his teeth clenched together as he waited for the moment to build.

"I got bumped up to animator."

Jimmy's face lit up. "Really? No way!"

"Yep. I'm finally going to be doing it full-time. Officially."

"Holy shit! That's amazing!" Jimmy leaned in to kiss him, taking Luke's hand in his own. "Babe, I am so happy for you. This is huge. How did it happen? We have to celebrate."

"I know. It's so unexpected. One of the new hires backed out at the last minute. I didn't know it at the time, but I guess

I was next in line and they're starting up on this project next week and need a full team."

"I told you they liked you! It was only a matter of time."

"There is a catch though."

Jimmy waited.

"The project is in California."

Jimmy's eyes widened. "So you have to go there to work on it?"

"Yes. San Diego."

"For how long?"

"Two months," Luke replied.

"Two months," Jimmy repeated, eyes peeled open.

They remained silent for a moment, staring, each waiting for the other to proceed. Worry settled into the space between them.

"I couldn't really say no," Luke added.

"No! Of course not." Jimmy regained his excitement. "This is huge. I'm so happy for you. Sure, I'll miss you, but two months isn't that long."

"It'll fly by," Luke concurred. He continued to explain the job to Jimmy and share every detail about his new promotion. Jimmy grew quiet. He had thought about being alone again, sometimes even craved that old, familiar life of solitude that was his for so many years. But now faced with the reality of that scenario, he froze. It wasn't missing Luke that troubled him, though he would surely miss the man he had come to love; it was the fear of what being apart would do to their already fragile foundation that caused him pause.

"Babe, you okay?" Luke asked.

"Yeah—yeah. I'm sorry," Jimmy replied as he started in on his salad.

"You're not going to go off and find another man while I'm away, are you?"

"Me? I'm the one that should be worried. All those laidback, California types—you'll be in heaven."

"Oh yeah, that's just what I'm after. A surfer dude."

"Well, maybe I can meet you over there and spend a weekend if it feels like the time is getting to us," Jimmy suggested.

"Yes! That would be perfect."

"When are you supposed to leave?"

"Monday."

Jimmy's mouth opened wide, bits of quinoa falling to his plate.

"Monday. Wow, that soon?"

"I know. Everyone else has known for months now, but since I was second-string it was all last minute."

"Well, hey—two months," Jimmy replied, shrugging off his concern. "That's eight weeks. Not so bad."

Luke smiled agreeably, eager to receive his lunch as it finally arrived.

"We have to celebrate!" Jimmy added. "This is huge."

Chapter Eighteen

JIMMY HURRIEDLY ARRANGED a get-together for Friday night, wrangling together most of Luke's friends to celebrate his promotion and bid him farewell. The small, basement dive bar reeked of booze and urine. The crowd was sparse, an eclectic mix of young drinkers seeking cheap alcohol. Doug arrived first, looking unusually put-away, with his new girlfriend—her positive influence already apparent. Jimmy spent some time talking to the new couple, genuinely curious about how they had met, discreetly trying to understand what exactly she saw in Doug. Soon after, Alex arrived followed by a group of Luke's more distant friends. Jimmy did his best to keep the group entertained, ordering drinks for people and catching up with friends he only barely knew. Luke arrived well after nine o'clock to a crowded bar, the group cheering as he entered like an overly enthused sitcom audience. Luke hollered back as he made his way to Jimmy.

"I started to think you weren't going to show," Jimmy said with relief.

"Sorry. We were prepping for the trip and it ran late. This is great," he said with a boyish smile, his excitement too large to contain. "How did you get everyone together?"

"A powerful little thing called the internet."

Jimmy escorted Luke through the crowd and ordered another round of beers for the small group that had gathered near the bar. Doug approached and pulled Luke in for a hug. Others congregated around the man of the hour. They congratulated, asked questions, joked about Luke learning to surf as the night waned on and Jimmy slipped away. He glided from group to group, playing host to the guests more loosely spread out around the bar, feigning interest in conversations he only partially understood. He had thought about inviting Charlie. An ally would be appreciated. But it was Luke's night. Jimmy had no desire to interfere.

Luke remained by the bar flanked by friends for most of the night. Jimmy kept an eye on him as he drifted around aimlessly. He watched as Luke enjoyed one beer after the next. His laughter grew louder, bouncing off the walls and filling the tight space. He went from talking loudly to shouting at the people around him. His speech began to slur the way it did whenever he overindulged. He held on to the counter, frailly maintaining his balance as he hollered at Doug with more and more zest. Jimmy questioned going over and offering his support, if for nothing else to prevent Luke from falling over, but his presence would remind Luke of appropriateness, dampen his fun. Luke deserved to celebrate freely.

By the time Doug and his girlfriend left, the last of the group to remain, Luke had quieted. Tiredness was settling in. His body swayed loosely from side to side. He looked around blankly at the nearly empty bar.

"I feel like I haven't seen you all night," he muttered as he wrapped his arms around Jimmy's waist, pressing him into the bar.

Jimmy finished closing the tab with the bartender and turned around. Luke's eyelids fluttered, fighting to stay open. His head struggled to stay erect.

"Looks like someone had a good time."

"I did," Luke whispered, his breath reeking of alcohol as he sloppily kissed Jimmy. "Thank you for this. You are the greatest."

"I'm glad you had fun."

"Did *you* have fun?" Luke asked. "Where were you all night?"

"I was around," Jimmy replied with a caring smile. "Are you about ready to go?"

"I think so. Everyone's cleared out, ha?"

"It appears so. Let's get you home."

Jimmy took Luke's arm and tossed it over his shoulder.

The street was quiet. Only a few night crawlers remained, creeping out of near empty bars, beginning their staggering journeys home. Luke freed himself from Jimmy once outside and bent down, resting his hands on his knees. He froze for a moment as Jimmy watched with concern.

"I think I'm gonna throw up," Luke mumbled.

Jimmy ran his hand up and down Luke's back. "It's okay if you need to. You might feel better if you do." He waited for a moment as Luke breathed heavily, hunched over like an exhausted runner. "Do you want to sit down for a minute?" Jimmy asked.

They took a seat on the curb just outside the bar, Jimmy guiding Luke carefully down to the concrete.

"We can just sit here for a minute," Jimmy offered, "until you feel good enough to walk."

"It's cold."

Jimmy smiled and tugged at the zipper on Luke's thin jacket. "It's just the breeze."

"I'm sorry I'm such a mess." Luke's head fell heavy onto Jimmy's shoulder. He reached over and grabbed Jimmy's hand, tightly locking fingers.

"Nothing to be sorry about," Jimmy replied. "It's your night. I'm glad you had fun."

"Did you have fun?" Luke asked again.

"Of course."

Jimmy peered down to the mix of fingers in his lap. Luke had started chewing his fingernails again. The edges appeared frayed the way they had years ago when they first met. Jimmy's thumb ran back and forth across the perimeter of the boyish fingers that somehow always seemed to fit together so comfortably with his own.

"Are you going to miss me?" Luke asked.

"Of course."

Jimmy kissed Luke's sweaty forehead and allowed his head to fall on Luke's. The nest of wavy hair provided a comforting resting place. His eyes closed as he enjoyed being silently linked together. It had been some time since they felt like one cohesive unit. Time had erected its own boundaries, dividing the two in unforeseen ways. He had almost forgotten what it felt like to be without those walls. There was a subtle peace in that fluidity, the lines between one and the next blurred beyond recognition.

"Sometimes I wonder if you really will miss me," Luke whispered. "Sometimes I wonder if you aren't actually looking forward to it."

"Why would you say that?" Jimmy asked. "Of course I'm not looking forward to it."

"Sometimes I wonder if you still love me."

Jimmy peeled his eyes open. His breath froze. It was unlike Luke to be so direct. His sadness became Jimmy's, filling him with remorse. Jimmy had, in fact, questioned it himself. There were, after all, times when he felt alone even in Luke's company, times when he worried Luke might never really hear him, or see him, or understand the vastness of what lay inside. But then that feeling would return, sparked by the simplest gesture or look—that feeling of joy that coursed through his body, comforting him like a knowing embrace. Of course he loved Luke. But sometimes he did question if that was enough.

"You're not thinking clearly," Jimmy said softly.

Luke lifted his head from Jimmy's shoulder.

Jimmy watched with concern. "Are you okay?" he asked. "You still feel like vomiting?"

"No," Luke replied. The fullness of his voice had returned. He straightened his back as he stared ahead. "I feel a little better," he noted as he turned and smiled at Jimmy.

"Take your time," Jimmy said, rubbing his back gently. "There's no rush."

"Yeah. Let's not hurry home. I haven't seen you all night." Luke's body slouched again as his head fell back into its old resting place. He took Jimmy's arm and draped it around his shoulder as he nestled closer. "Do you remember that seedy hotel room near Gramercy?"

Jimmy smiled brightly.

"This bar kinda smelled like it," Luke continued.

Jimmy laughed. "I guess so. Like sweat and booze."

"I was so hot for you," Luke added.

"Was?"

"Still am."

"We had sex all day," Jimmy noted.

"I know," Luke replied. "I remember everything about it—the way your hair looked, the way you smelled and tasted. I remember the way you looked at me. It was the first time I could tell we were feeling the same thing. It put my mind at ease."

"You didn't know that before?"

"No," Luke replied. "I couldn't read you before. Sometimes I thought I was safe, but then you'd act a certain way or say something that would throw me off and I would doubt myself all over again."

Jimmy struggled to remember what he had been like back then, how he had acted, what he had done or said to make Luke question his affections. Most of his apparent indifference was likely just masked insecurity. He, too, had worried his feelings might not be reciprocated. Any sign of disinterest was merely self-preservation.

"It's strange to think that was actually not that long ago," Jimmy said.

"It feels so distant, doesn't it? I wanted to squeeze you to death. Wrap my arms around you and suffocate you."

Jimmy laughed, recalling that feeling with distinct clarity. "We stayed in that bed all day. Glued together by sweat."

"It was perfect." Luke dug his head into Jimmy's shoulder, pressing closer though there was no distance left to close. "We should take a trip. Go somewhere different."

'That would be fun," Jimmy replied.

"Let's do it. When I come back."

"Okay. It's a date. Let's maybe find a better hotel, though."

"I'll leave that part to you."

"Probably best."

Jimmy let his head fall once more onto Luke's as he watched a cab zoom past on the otherwise bare street. The streetlight above flickered, struggling to stay lit, illuminating the two boys alone on the empty sidewalk, their bodies woven together. Luke's breathing rose and fell, steady and heavy as though he had already fallen asleep. Its calming rhythm had become a familiar drone, most nights easing Jimmy into a peaceful rest. He would miss its comfort.

Chapter Nineteen

THE HARDEST PART about Luke being away came at the end of the day. The bed felt empty without him. Jimmy tossed and turned, trying to quiet his restless mind. His body had grown accustomed to Luke's. It had reduced itself to only half of the equation, rendered useless without the other half. Jimmy was fine the rest of the day—happy, even. But nights were hard.

When Charlie suggested they go out, Jimmy seized the opportunity to drink away his worries. Maybe being drunk was exactly what he needed to finally get a good night's rest.

The bar was packed. Saturday night in full swing. Go-go dancers hung from beams attached to the ceiling like kids on monkey bars—except nearly naked, with perfectly toned bodies, and skin dripping in oil. It had been some time since Jimmy had been in a place like this. It wasn't really Luke's thing. Truthfully, it wasn't really Jimmy's anymore either, but a night out seemed like it might help.

"So you're happy he's gone?" Charlie asked, confused and struggling to hear in the crowded space.

"No. That's what I'm trying to explain," Jimmy shouted. "There are parts about being alone again that I really appreciate. But then I get this sinking feeling whenever I'm ready for bed and I remember he's not around. I miss him. So much more than I thought I would."

Charlie shot him a sympathetic look and signaled Jimmy to finish his drink. Jimmy complied, chugged the last of his vodka tonic, and followed Charlie to the dance floor. He dove into the sea of men where sweaty bodies grinded together, becoming one with the freely swaying mass, and allowed himself to be tossed back and forth by strangers, getting swept away by waves of pleasure and excitement.

Charlie got lost in the crowd, but Jimmy was too entranced to worry. His eyes rolled back and shut as he abandoned the surrounding world, sights and sounds all merging into the darkness cast by the backs of his eyelids. He floated there, in a beautiful nothingness, as time passed unnoticeably. When he finally opened his eyes, he noticed the sheer vastness of the space. Above was a second-floor balcony that wrapped around the perimeter of the dance floor. Men lined the rails, peering down, examining their many options in the sea of drunk and drugged dancers. Luke would have hated this place.

"This is what's wrong with gay guys," he might've said. "Always looking for their next fuck."

He wouldn't have been far off base, Jimmy thought. But it was fun. There was no denying that. Jimmy hadn't, in fact, had this much fun in longer than he cared to remember. The rush of bare skin and sweat, alcohol and bass was intoxicating. It was a relief to surrender to it. He wondered if any of the strange men had been watching him. Perhaps he had gained the attention of a seedy onlooker or two.

"Jimmy!" Charlie shouted. "I have to pee!"

"Hey!" Jimmy shouted back, delighted to be reunited with his friend, though in the time that had passed he had largely forgotten about Charlie entirely. "Me too!"

He allowed Charlie to pull him out of the crowd as his senses returned to reality. They entered a cylindrical hallway fully illuminated in alternating shades of pink and purple. The space between him and Charlie widened as they made their way to the bathroom. Shadows of dancing men lined the translucent walls. The tempting silhouettes captured Jimmy's attention as he made his way through the cavernous passageway. Crowds gathered near small holes in the wall about waist high. Jimmy slowed his pace further to examine what was going on. Curiously, he approached one of the vacant dancers, a seductively swaying shadow figure hidden behind the frosted barrier. A small curtain covered the hole in front of the dancer, a thin obstruction between Jimmy and the unseen seducer. He stared at it, imagining what wonders lay behind. Suddenly, the curtain parted and the mysterious dancer's arm extended out, gesturing for his hand. He gladly gave it, allowing the shadow to guide his hand through the hole.

The stranger's semi-erect shaft was thick and fleshy, slippery with grease. Jimmy allowed his fingers to wrap around the impressive mass as it throbbed in his grasp. His eyes closed as he basked in the joy of the real life wet dream, almost too spontaneously erotic to be true. He began to stroke it as it throbbed more intensely. Its size was unreal, begging for further examination. A rush of excitement filled him as he felt the dancer's enthusiasm growing larger and larger. He allowed his hand to caress every inch of the stranger's member, feeling every vein and curve, creating a mental image strong enough for him to retain once the alcohol had worn off and he had regained his sober senses. Still, it wasn't enough. He longed to see what was in his possession. He bent down, boldly parting the curtain to reveal the giant, veiny cock, but only caught a glimpse before it pulled away from his grasp. He was interrupted by a heavyset man in a skin-tight black T-shirt.

"Okay, you've had your fun," the bouncer said. "Keep it moving."

Jimmy removed his hand from the now vacant cubbyhole and stepped away from the wall, proudly wiping it clean across his jeans as he continued down the hallway, eventually reaching the endless bathroom line.

Charlie was nowhere in sight. He braced against the wall as he waited, thoughts of the stranger's penis still filling his head with excitement. He felt a rush of accomplishment as he reviewed the events of the night, grateful that he had discovered this bizarre new venue. Maybe he would bring Luke one day. If he was drunk enough, they might actually have some fun. After an endless wait, Jimmy arrived at the front of the line, his bladder demanding release. The door swung open and he scurried forward, eager to enter, when suddenly he was cut off. A man rushed in, leaping past Jimmy and bypassing the line entirely. Jimmy stormed into the bathroom directly after the stranger as the door slammed shut.

"What the fuck!" he shouted, ready to correct the injustice.

"I have to pee," said the man.

"We all do!" Jimmy barked back. "That's why there's a line! You can't just run up in here, jumping in front of everyone and expect..."

Jimmy began to notice the man in the midst of his rant. He was by all observable accounts a typical, overconfident alpha male, probably in his midforties, overly obsessed with working out and manicuring his eyebrows. His skin was rough, but hairless with a not-so subtle orange hue, the obvious result of too much tanning. He was trashy hot. Attractive in a universally understandable sort of way, but of a type Jimmy had never fancied. He wore a button-down, short-sleeve shirt with only a few buttons actually fastened toward the bottom, leaving his bulging chest exposed.

Despite his preferences, Jimmy could not help but to appreciate the severity of the man's build. His toned muscles created a hard line in the center of his chest, so severe it looked like it hurt. Sweat sat like varnish along the harsh crevice leading deeper into his shirt.

"Listen," the man interjected, crushing Jimmy's resolve with his unexpected tranquility. "I'm sorry. Just go ahead and pee. I'll wait here."

The man stepped back to the corner of the bathroom, away from the toilet and sink, and geared his attention to his phone. Jimmy was surprised by the ease with which the rude stranger had remedied the situation. His solution seemed reasonable enough, and he had, after all, apologized.

Jimmy made his way to the toilet, ready to unzip his pants when he noticed the giant mirrored wall in front of him. His reflection stared back, his hand stationed at his crotch. *What a strange design choice*, he thought. As he continued to unzip he glanced to the right of his reflection and spotted the stranger's reflection as he waited behind, presently preoccupied with his phone but only a glance away from watching Jimmy pee. Jimmy abandoned the toilet and marched over to the man in the corner, grabbing a hold of his bulging biceps as he spun him around without a word. The stunned stranger chuckled, watching Jimmy as he involuntarily turned to face the wall. His arms were rock solid, their girth too wide for Jimmy to fully wrap his hands around.

The man reached behind and grabbed Jimmy's ass.

"Oh," he moaned. "Forceful, are we?"

Jimmy laughed as he spotted the hint of a tattoo on the back of the man's neck peeking up above his shirt collar. He hadn't realized how short the man was before. Jimmy towered above him as he stood behind, the tip of his nose reaching the top of the man's head. The stranger took hold of Jimmy's arms and wrapped them around his torso allowing his head to fall back onto Jimmy's shoulder as their bodies began swaying gently side to side, the two unexpectedly engaged in a hypnotic dance, the muffled bass seeping in through the bathroom door providing a pulse to their movement. Jimmy could feel himself harden despite his better judgment as his crotch grazed lightly across the man's back. The man's warm breath ran across Jimmy's neck as he moaned. It smelled of peppermint. He began to kiss Jimmy's neck, working his way up to his cheeks until their lips met.

Jimmy quickly pulled away, but the man grabbed him, pressing his chest against Jimmy's as his mouth opened wide. His hand rested at the back of Jimmy's head, holding him in place. Despite his short stature, his grip was firm and commanding. Jimmy teetered back and forth—kissing back, then pulling away. With each step back, the man followed, his tongue swirling wildly in Jimmy's mouth until they moved all the way to the other end of the bathroom and Jimmy backed into the sink counter near the toilet. The man grabbed Jimmy's hips and with little effort hoisted him onto the counter. Jimmy's legs, as if possessed by an intent all their own, wrapped around the man's torso as his mouth opened wide. They kissed frantically, as if on borrowed time. The man tasted like mint and cigarettes. It was almost revolting, the strange flavor, but there was something about its foreignness that was intoxicating, fueling Jimmy with an overwhelming desire. He surrendered his resistance and consumed the strange man, a mess of saliva and heavy breathing lulling him into a hazy trance.

A loud pound shook the bathroom door.

"Hurry the fuck up!" a muffled voice shouted.

Jimmy pried his lips from the man and pushed him away, returning to his senses, almost immediately regretful.

The man chuckled as he approached again, ready to pounce.

"I have to go," Jimmy said sharply as he jumped off the counter.

"We're just getting started," the stranger said. He inched closer, staring at Jimmy, the sides of his mouth wet with saliva.

Jimmy shook his head in disbelief and shuffled away, swinging the bathroom door open.

"What the fuck! Come on!" the man shouted as Jimmy bolted out of the bathroom, the door closing behind him.

Jimmy traveled through the neon-colored hallway, past the wall of shadowed dancers, heading for the exit. He spotted Charlie at the end of the hallway. The strobe of lights from the distant dance floor cast a halo around his friend's slight frame. He appeared almost angelic. The hallway shortened as the image of Charlie became clearer. Jimmy rushed over to him, relieved.

"What the fuck!" Charlie shouted, slapping Jimmy's arm. "You keep running off."

"Sorry. I was in the bathroom." It was all too unreal to discuss, too heated to even wrap his head around. Jimmy even questioned for a moment if it had happened at all. Perhaps, he thought, he had imagined the whole thing.

"Are you okay?" Charlie asked.

"Yeah," Jimmy replied, wiping the scene from his memory as quickly as it had happened. "Let's get out of here."

Chapter Twenty

JIMMY BEGAN TO fall asleep with greater ease as he slipped into a routine not unlike the one he followed when he was single. But Luke's absence was still felt. He distracted himself as best he could, but it was impossible to ignore the unsettled feeling that crept up whenever he thought of him. He hadn't anticipated missing Luke as much as he did, but his world felt empty without him. He spent time with Charlie and Michael, he visited his parents in Long Island, but nothing sufficed to fill the void. It was not being alone that bothered Jimmy; he was good at being alone. It was Luke and his puffy eyes, his crooked smile, his shaggy hair that Jimmy missed. He longed to hold him again, to feel his smooth skin pressed against his own. There were times when Jimmy could taste Luke in his mouth, smell him in the room. It plagued him with guilt to remember a time, so recent, when he questioned leaving, throwing it all away for some grandiose idea of freedom whereby he might find something more perfect than what he had already gained. Things would be different, he promised himself as he returned home with a box of cupcakes. He would be different.

Jimmy scurried into the kitchen, digging around for some time before finding the ceramic cake stand he had in mind. He neatly arranged the cupcakes on the stand and rested it on the new table, careful not to mar its glistening surface. He had found the small, round kitchen table lying on its side in an alleyway while walking to the office. The walnut wood and dainty, midcentury form immediately caught his eye. It was, however, fairly weathered, scrapes and dings covering most of the top, but he was certain that with a little effort it would be the perfect new addition to the apartment. Michael had helped him lug it home after work. It took two rejections before they found a cab willing to take on the task. Restoring it was a quicker project than he had anticipated. After a bit of light sanding and staining, it was as good as new. The kitchen cabinets came soon after. The dark finish of the drab wood had always bothered him. Now with the new table, he thought it time to give the ugly cabinets an overhaul. It took an entire weekend to apply the light-gray paint. He worked with care, removing the hardware and getting into every nook and cranny with meticulous precision. He had been disappointed by Luke's lack of interest when he finally revealed the new kitchen to him during one of their late-night video calls, but Luke was busy. More pressing matters were on his mind, bigger than Jimmy's largely unnecessary home-improvement projects.

Luke returned home to a candlelit apartment. A homemade *Welcome Home* banner hung on the wall near the TV. Dinner lay neatly spread out on the shimmering wooden table, the cake stand full of cupcakes acting as the centerpiece. They hugged as soon as Luke entered, remaining in each other's embrace for some time. Luke held Jimmy's face, examining him before their lips met with an eager familiarity, not wanting to separate for long.

"I am so happy to be home," Luke said softly.

"I'm happy to have you back," Jimmy replied. "You look slimmer."

"No time to eat."

Luke dropped his bag to the floor and shut the door.

"I know, it sounded crazy."

"It was intense," Luke said as he wandered around the apartment as if to remind himself of the space. "I love the candles," he noted with a bright smile, filling the apartment again with his beaming grin. "How romantic. And you made dinner! Babe, it looks amazing."

"Just some pasta. Nothing fancy."

Luke made his way to the kitchen, touching the freshly painted cabinets as he passed. "This looks great. Nice job."

"Thanks. I'm pretty happy with it."

He seemed almost like a foreigner, traversing the space unknowingly. Luke roamed, his hands gliding across the surface of the cabinets and counter, assessing everything that had changed since his last visit. He stopped at the new table and hovered over it for a moment, peering down at its surface with intrigue.

"You said you found this in the dumpster?" he asked.

"It was sitting by the trash near our office."

"I would have never thought to pick it up, but it really does fit nicely. How did you manage to get it home?"

"Michael helped," Jimmy replied. "It was hard to find a cabbie willing to drive us to Queens with a giant table in the trunk, but we made it work."

Luke's eyes darted forward. "He was here?" he asked.

"Yeah. Thankfully. There was no way I would've been able to lug it up the stairs on my own."

The small gap between Luke's eyebrows closed as he squinted. "But he came into the apartment?"

"Well, yeah," Jimmy replied, taken aback by Luke's sudden concern. "How else would we have gotten it in here?"

"You didn't tell me he was here when we talked."

"I didn't?"

"No."

"Why does it matter?" Jimmy asked.

Luke sighed sarcastically and rolled his eyes. He worked his fingers across the table's surface, bending down to scrutinize every inch, suddenly more interested in the new piece of furniture. He circumvented the foreign object as if to find some clue hidden beneath its surface, a part of the story Jimmy was leaving out.

"Seems like a big favor to ask," he noted calmly, his investigation still underway.

"He offered," Jimmy replied with an equal dose of forced nonchalance. "We both agreed it was too good of a find to leave out on the street."

"That's really nice of him." Luke stood tall, his attention now aimed at Jimmy like he was waiting for a confession.

Jimmy stared back defiantly, offended by Luke's silent accusation but trying hard to maintain peace. "Shall we eat?" he suggested.

Dinner was spent catching up. Luke spoke of a party the team had thrown on their last night in San Diego, an informal celebration to commemorate the end of the seemingly difficult project. He shared details of the new friends he had made along the way. Jimmy was pleased to hear they were a welcoming group, accepting Luke as part of the creative team without reservation. When they finished eating they sank into the couch, easing into each other as effortlessly as they always had. Luke held Jimmy tightly, kissing the side of his neck as their bare feet rubbed together like hands keeping warm.

"You smell so good," Luke whispered.

"I just showered."

"I'm sure I reek from hours of crammed travel."

"You smell like you." Jimmy breathed him in. "I like it." He had missed that scent, the warmth of his touch.

"I bet you enjoyed having the place to yourself for a little while."

"It wasn't so bad," Jimmy replied. "I got used to it after a while, in spite of missing you as much as I did."

"Did you really miss me?" Luke asked.

"More than you know. Did you miss *me*?"

"Every day." Luke kissed Jimmy's neck again, working his way up to his ear where he nibbled gently on the tender bit of flesh. "Did you get to spend some time with Charlie?" he asked.

"Yeah. We hung out a little." Jimmy's heart skipped a beat as he pushed the memory of the bathroom incident out of his mind. Remembering it made him shudder, so he resigned to pretending it never happened. After all, it was a harmless, drunken mistake hidden away behind closed doors. As long as he denied it strongly enough, he might actually begin to believe it was only imagined.

Luke worked his hand into Jimmy's shirt, caressing his stomach while he continued pecking at his neck and shoulder. Jimmy sighed, his skin thrilled to be touched. They made love on the sofa, slowly and methodically, not unlike their first time. Luke was cautious when he entered, careful not to hurt Jimmy. Their noses lightly grazed as their lips hovered close. Jimmy's gaze remained fixed on Luke throughout, taking in every detail as if seeing him for the first time—the dark circles around his eyes, his long, pointed nose. Jimmy would never find anyone more beautiful than he did Luke.

Chapter Twenty-One

MICHAEL BEAMED WITH excitement as he said goodbye to Jimmy.

"Are you sure you'll be okay on your own for the next couple days?" he asked, unable to restrain his smile.

"I got it," Jimmy replied confidently. "Don't worry about a thing."

"Okay, but call me if anything comes up. I can always shoot back over here."

"Relax. Enjoy your weekend."

It was only Wednesday, but Michael was starting his weekend early, taking a trip to Montauk with his new love interest. They'd met only three weeks prior, but things seemed to be escalating quickly. Jimmy enjoyed watching his coworker transform into such a positive force. The entire office seemed to lighten, Michael's mood somehow contagious. He was quick to leave work as early as he could each night, entrusting Jimmy with more responsibility.

Despite his growing influence at the company, Jimmy began to feel restless at Freestyle. Being an accounts manager of sorts fell tragically short of where he hoped to land in his career. In many ways he envied Luke, who spent most of his days being creative. He was, of course, happy for his impassioned boyfriend who seemed more enlivened since returning home, but it was difficult at times to maintain his enthusiasm while his own career path seemed to hit a roadblock.

He gathered his things shortly after Michael boarded the elevator, eager to return home to Luke while there was still time to make the most of the evening. Maybe they could catch a movie or walk in the park and admire the evening's pink glow, the waning sun setting eclectic Astoria ablaze in a wash of warm, coziness. Really, he hoped they'd fuck. Lately, he found it hard to keep his hands off Luke. They made love against the kitchen counter, on the sofa, in the shower, wherever the urge struck. Luke was all smiles, appreciative of Jimmy's abnormally unquenchable thirst, always ready to please and be pleased.

Jimmy arrived home to an apartment in disarray. He had managed, lately, to stop himself from nagging, allowing Luke to toss his clothes wherever he wanted, to leave unwashed dishes piled precariously in the sink. It's not that it didn't bother him. It did. But he was determined to focus on the positive. What did it matter if he still had to leap over a half-unpacked suitcase and a pile of Luke's sneakers to make it to the bed when their lovemaking was as heated as it had been? Surely Jimmy could ignore a little mess if it made Luke feel more at home. After all, a clean apartment without Luke paled in comparison to a messy apartment with him. He would, however, tidy up just a bit, he decided as he picked up a half-eaten bowl of cold cereal sitting on the coffee table. By the time Luke returned home from work, the apartment was spotless, back to its original Jimmy-approved level of tidiness.

"You cleaned up," Luke noted as he took his shoes off with extra care. "Sorry, babe. I could've helped if you waited."

"I got home early anyway. It gave me something to do."

Luke leaped onto the couch, leaving space for Jimmy to join. "Michael's been a lot easier on you lately."

Jimmy willingly obliged, his body sinking into Luke's like wax into a mold. "He's been in a good mood since he met his latest fling."

"He's dating someone?" Luke asked. "I didn't know that."

"I didn't tell you? It's been a little while now."

"Well, looks like you missed your chance."

Luke kissed the back of Jimmy's neck. Jimmy's eyes rolled back as he held on to Luke's arm, draped snuggly around him. They pushed and pulled at each other. Their bodies burrowed into one another until Jimmy turned around to face him. He jutted his tongue forward, working with snakelike prowess as Luke opened his mouth wider. Jimmy ran his hand up Luke's chest and up to his smooth, clean-shaven cheek. Luke grabbed a hold of Jimmy's back.

"Is that why you've been extra revved up lately?" Luke asked between kisses.

"What does that mean?" Jimmy asked, as he retracted his tongue.

"Nothing." Luke swallowed hard. "I'm just kidding." He pushed his knee between Jimmy's, weaving their legs together as he leaned forward and pecked at Jimmy's lips.

Jimmy kissed back, but Luke's question echoed in his mind. He pulled away, opening the space between them.

"Why would Michael have anything to do with us?" Jimmy asked.

Luke grinned, rubbing his nose against Jimmy's as he took a breath. "I was just messing around."

"But what are you trying to say exactly?"

"About what?"

"Michael."

"Nothing. I'm sorry I said anything." Luke leaned forward, again trying to kiss an all-too-preoccupied Jimmy. "Come on. What's wrong?"

"Do you really think we've been having more sex lately because I'm upset about Michael?"

"No. I was just kidding."

Jimmy glared at Luke with disbelief.

Luke sighed exhaustedly, throwing his head against the sofa. Something seemed to be on his mind, but he hesitated to express it. They sat in silence, a familiar tension suspended between them as Luke gathered his thoughts. "Trust me," he began. "I'm not complaining. But you've been—" He paused. "Different since I got back."

Jimmy's agitation turned to concern. Panic filled him as his eyes wandered, searching for a way out.

"Not bad-different," Luke explained further. "Just different."

"I'm just happy you're home," Jimmy replied, regretful he had encouraged the conversation. "I missed you."

"I know. Of course. And I'm happy to be back too. But you have to admit, something feels off. Like things aren't quite where we left them."

Jimmy shimmied slightly farther away from Luke. He had hoped they might remain ignorant to the reasons why things were suddenly different. They were, after all, better. "Yeah, but isn't that a good thing?" he asked. "We're not fighting all the time."

"But *you* feel different."

Luke stared at Jimmy. His gaze was soft, but it bore past the surface, peering deep inside. Jimmy sat up. He thought of a dozen things he could say to appease Luke. Not all of them would be lies. He could explain how being apart made him realize what he had, how he was reminded of what he had somehow stopped seeing—that perfect something that had been in front of him this whole time. He could explain how he had grown instantly grateful for all the things he had perhaps taken for granted. He could tell Luke how he had longed for his flesh and was eager to devour it now that he had the chance. But he couldn't run away from the catalyst of this sudden realization, that tiny indiscretion he hoped to forget. Despite his best efforts, he couldn't push it out of his mind. It continually seeped its way into his thoughts, that stomach-churning taste of peppermint and cigarettes, festering in the corner of his memory like months-old garbage, the stench of it too sickening to bear. Jimmy's eyes widened as the space around him narrowed. Words rose like vomit barreling through his throat. "Listen," he uttered, partly hoping he might stop himself in his own tracks before continuing further. "There's something I need to tell you, but I don't want you to freak out."

Luke sat up carefully, his gaze fixed on Jimmy. His breath froze as he waited, suspicion growing in his eyes as silence prevailed.

"Remember the night I went out with Charlie? I told you we went to that crazy gay club with the go-go dancers?"

Luke nodded, his brow weighing heavy over his puffy eyes.

"Something happened that night," Jimmy continued, his eyes filling to the brim as he aimed for the truth. "But it was nothing. And I was really drunk." He glanced at Luke who sat frozen, silently staring, worry plastered on his already-wounded face. Jimmy looked away, unable to make eye contact as he relived the events of that night—the intoxicating rush of floating on the dance floor, the feeling of a shadow-dancer's erection in his hands. He was careful to cast the bathroom stranger as an unappealing, one-dimensional buffoon, the kind of guy he would never imagine doing anything with had he not been drunk beyond reason. He told Luke how it happened, the kiss hitting him by surprise, the stranger eager to engage. "We just kissed," Jimmy assured him. "And as soon as I realized what I was doing, I ran out of there."

Luke shook his head as his paleness filled with that familiar redness. Jimmy glanced at him for a moment, but averted his attention.

A silent tension filled the air, uncertainty dangling between them.

"Are you fucking serious?" Luke shouted as he sprang up from the couch. He looked down at Jimmy in shock.

Jimmy peered up, nearly fearful of what Luke might do. Tears dripped from his eyes as he watched Luke, red with anger.

"I honestly don't know what happened," Jimmy murmured, out of breath with panic. "One minute I was yelling at him for jumping the line and the next we were kissing."

Luke scoffed as he backed away and began to pace back and forth across the living room. "And that was it?" he asked, his gaze filled with rage. "You *accidentally* kissed, then left?"

"Yes," Jimmy replied.

"Did you want to fuck him?"

"No! Not at all. I didn't even find him attractive in the least. It was just a knee-jerk reaction. As soon as I realized what I was doing, I left."

"Come on, man!" Luke shouted, his arms flailing as he turned away from Jimmy. He moved to the corner of the living room, his head lowered like a boy in timeout. "I knew something was up," he murmured. He remained still, his back to Jimmy. Jimmy waited silently, too scared to get up or make a move of any kind. "You've got to be fucking kidding me!" Luke shouted, and bolted to the kitchen.

Jimmy sat motionless on the couch as he heard the fridge door open and slam shut. Cabinet doors followed. Minutes passed, the wall between the kitchen and living room separating the two.

"Babe, please," Jimmy pleaded as he meekly stood up. "Talk to me."

"Now you want to fucking talk," Luke barked. "You've been lying to me for weeks! I have to admit, I was worried when I left, but I never thought you'd be so fucking stupid." Jimmy apologized again and again, trying his best to convey just how insignificant it all was without trying to justify his actions. "I'm sure you loved it," Luke interrupted from behind the kitchen wall. "Don't act like it was all some accident. I'm sure you wanted his cock inside you. Who's to say it wasn't?"

"Luke. Come on."

"Charlie was probably egging you on, wasn't he? The little shit." Jimmy grew quiet, biting hard at his lip to hold back tears as Luke fired off one painful insult after the next. Jimmy silently winced in pain as the blows continued. Luke's tone was sharp and spiteful. He could be hurtful when he wanted to be, but Jimmy had before only witnessed hints of his aggression. Nothing like this. Jimmy's hands began to shake until the vibration rose to his arms and chest, his whole body pulsating. He reminded himself that he had, in fact, been an idiot. He deserved to be slighted. Anything Luke needed to do or say was fair enough.

Eventually, Luke stopped. Jimmy could hear him heaving, out of breath. The last of his ammunition had been used up.

"You had to go shit all over things," he said with a heavy sigh, his voice finally quieting. "Now what am I supposed to do?"

A moment of silence befell them before Luke emerged from the kitchen. Their eyes made four, pain reflecting sorrow. Jimmy longed to rush in and hug him, to assure him everything was going to be okay, to wrap his arms around Luke and put out the fire. He waited for a sign, some indication that it might be safe to approach. Luke gave none. Jimmy breathed heavy and inched forward, one tiny step at a time. The blankness of Luke's expression was chilling. He stood motionless near the table, gaze fixed as Jimmy carefully closed the gap between them. When Jimmy was finally within arm's reach, Luke lowered his head. It swayed back and forth, dangling in disbelief.

"Fuck this," he murmured.

His legs took flight. He rammed his shoulder into Jimmy as he bolted past. Jimmy spun around, struggling to keep his feet planted as Luke stormed out of the apartment, slamming the door shut with a thud that shook the living room. Books fell from shelves. The walls shivered. The tremble traveled through the floorboards and reached Jimmy, stirring his insides further. He stood frozen in shock, his feet now cemented to the floor, the aftermath of the quake still ringing in his ear. He gasped in disbelief. His eyes wandered aimlessly around the apartment as he struggled to make sense of what had so quickly transpired. Tension still filled the empty space, thick like molasses, as countless minutes passed. He could feel its clutches rising up his motionless legs toward his hips, pulling him under, nearly drowning. "Fuck!" he finally shouted as he leaped into action.

He darted to the closet, grabbed Luke's jacket as he thrust on his own, and ran for the front door, fleeing the threatening space.

The neighborhood was quiet when he stormed out of the building. Enough time had passed that Luke could be anywhere. The sidewalks were empty. Heavy, metal shutters came crashing down over storefronts and businesses. The neon sign from the bakery across the street shut off with a flicker as the doors to the shop closed. Jimmy picked a direction and started running. He ran past the train station where a handful of commuters emerged, shuffling out of the way as he bore past. He crossed the nearly empty street, flying past the library and turning the corner. The block ahead was empty. He could see for what seemed like miles— not a soul in sight.

He turned around, wasting no time to retrace his steps, zooming past the apartment again as he continued his search across the other end of the neighborhood. He passed restaurants and closed cafés, his head darting back and forth in either direction, peering into street corners and alleyways as he flew by. Sweat dripped from every pore, his heart pounding like an erratic drum. He ran like a victim being chased, using every bit of energy to save himself from some impending doom until his body finally gave up. When he arrived at the park, he came to a screeching halt, tumbling to the ground, his legs loose like rubber. He panted for air on all fours. The grass was wet beneath his palms. It cooled his overheated body. Eventually he fell back to sit on his legs. Tears flowed in defeat as he sat alone in the desolate park.

The search was hopeless. Luke was gone. Maybe he had hopped on the train. Maybe he was riding it aimlessly, maybe he was heading to Doug's. Maybe he would return home before the night's end, maybe he wouldn't. Jimmy rested his head in his wet palms, sealing his eyes shut as he struggled to catch his breath. He fought the urge to wail, to scream recklessly into the lonely night. He swallowed hard, determined to stop the flow of tears. It was, after all, his own doing, this mess that he now found himself in. What right did he have to lament over its inevitable unraveling? He sealed his eyelids, squeezing them together with such force he began to wonder if the wet trail dripping down his cheeks might be blood. All the better if it was, he resolved. He deserved to be out of breath and bleeding. He had it coming.

When he finally opened his eyes, he hoped he might wake up in his room and come to find that the whole episode was nothing more than a bad dream. Maybe Luke would be in bed waiting for him, his lanky legs draped over the covers. Maybe they would kiss and fuck and hold each other as they slept. It was, however, the empty park that greeted him as his eyelids lifted. He was blocks away from home, crying in the soggy grass. The park was covered in darkness but for the dim, yellow light cast by the streetlamp across the way. He leaned his head back, looking up to the still night sky, and took a deep breath, collecting himself as he rose to his feet. He brushed grass and mud off his jeans and picked up Luke's jacket as he prepared himself for the walk home. Just as he was about to turn away from the desolate scene in front of him, he spotted something familiar. He squinted, drying his eyes with his hands as he focused more sharply on the mop of shaggy hair sitting alone on a bench in the far-off distance. A car headlight flicked on and off, casting a subtle glow around the loose, disheveled curls. Jimmy's heart stopped pounding for a moment, suspended in his chest.

He approached the bench with trepidation, unsure of what he was seeing as he crossed the long stretch of empty grass. Perhaps, he thought, his emotions had gotten the best of him, creating the false image like a mirage in the desert. But as he drew near, he became more certain. There was no mistaking those familiar, dark locks of wild, unmanaged hair.

Luke's attention remained fixed ahead as Jimmy approached, seeming so lost in thought he was barely aware of his surroundings. When Jimmy arrived, he meekly stepped in front of the lonely figure. Luke's body was stiff with discomfort, all the rage drained out of him as he sat, lost in a haze. His arms were crossed. He hugged himself tightly, fending off the night's chill. Jimmy extended his arm, offering Luke his jacket.

Luke's attention drifted toward Jimmy as he came out of his trance, but his weary eyes refused to meet Jimmy's. He took the jacket without a word. Jimmy swallowed hard, mustering up whatever strength he had left to prevent himself from crumpling. He waited for a moment before taking a seat on the bench, careful not to get too close. Out of the corner of his eye, Luke fumbled with his jacket. His body seemed too frail to manage. He struggled to get one arm in at a time and eventually fastened the misaligned buttons. When he finally settled into the jacket, Jimmy reached over to free its trapped collar. Luke allowed Jimmy to adjust it, raising it to stand tall and cover his neck. When it was properly set, Jimmy returned to his side of the bench, gaze falling on the darkness that lay ahead, happy to sit, even in silence, near Luke.

A headlight flicked on again, illuminating for a moment the swing set and slide that bordered the sidewalk. A woman emerged from her car, slammed the door shut, and locked it. The lights turned off and Jimmy and Luke returned to darkness.

"Did I break anything?" Luke asked, his voice low and groggy.

Jimmy turned to him, elated to hear his voice.

Luke stared ahead. "I slammed the door pretty hard."

Jimmy chuckled, tears in his eyes. "No. You didn't break anything. You did probably scare the neighbors, though."

Luke seemed to hold back amusement with a sigh, though even the tiniest glimmer of his grin excited Jimmy. That grin that he had come to know so well.

They returned to silence. Jimmy smiled as he peered down at his sneakers. They resembled Luke's—covered in mud, dirty and beaten. The crisp shine of newness had vanished, lessons learned stamped across its surface. But that's the thing with sneakers; the only way to keep them clean is to never really use them.

Jimmy would never be able to wipe clean the mess he had made of things just as he would never be able to forget what it felt like to be held by Luke, or feel his breath against his neck. But it was up to Luke to determine what his fate would be.

"You know, it's funny," Luke uttered, his voice gradually returning to its normal cadence. "When you love someone you also kinda hate them."

Jimmy grinned, his lips trembling in fear of the oncoming verdict.

"But that's just how it goes," Luke continued. "We don't waste our time hating people we don't give a shit about."

"Do you hate me?" Jimmy asked.

"Sometimes I think I do. And you hate me sometimes too." Luke turned to face Jimmy. "That's why you kissed that jerk, isn't it?"

Jimmy's head fell. "Maybe," he whispered. "In a way."

"You've been hating me for a while now."

"I don't hate you. I love you. I just got caught up in my head. I stopped seeing things clearly."

Luke's voice grew tender. "Are you *happy* with me?"

Jimmy raised his head. Their eyes finally connected. "More so than I even realized."

Luke's expression softened. His heavy eyebrows relaxed. They stared into each other as moments passed unnoticed. The night grew colder, but they remained, finally seeing each other clearly. Like the sky after it rains, the air was crisp and clear, filled only by that something that had always existed between them.

Luke looked away, sniffling as he gained his strength and inched toward Jimmy. Jimmy carefully shuffled nearer, closing the distance little by little until the edges of their pinkies met. A wave of warmth charged through Jimmy's hand, up his arm, straight to his chest. He allowed his eyes to shut, surrendering himself to the tiniest of touches. If it were to be his last, he intended to savor it. Luke lifted his hand and moved it over. Jimmy opened his palm to receive Luke's. Their fingers locked together as they remained silent, staring into the vast darkness that lay ahead.

Chapter Twenty-Two

JIMMY HAD PREPARED himself to be taken over by an immediate assault on the senses, imagining a scene of chaos and confusion. The airport was, however, unexpectedly bland. He walked through the desolate terminal, surprised by how familiar everything seemed. It could have been any airport in America with clusters of screens flickering an ever-changing array of flight statuses, towering glass windows, and automated walkways. The only indication he was in India came from the multilingual signs perfectly placed in the impressively modern New Delhi airport, directional aids pointing out bathrooms and exits in Hindi, English, and Urdu. The posters scattered along the walls resembled the ads that lined the sides of buildings and bus stations in his own city. Except, instead of smiling American faces, these were filled with the pleasant grins of Indian men and women. Some were dressed in Western clothing, others adorned more traditional wear, but each followed the same format of most any poster he had ever seen.

The familiarity of it all was both disappointing and comforting. He had expected it would be vastly different from his own world, but so far it seemed like a culturally appropriated version of the same thing. He drifted along the automated walkway in what appeared to be India's answer to JFK airport, the faint sound of a Kenny G–like instrumental track filling the already uninspiring space with an added dose of uneventfulness.

A group had formed near one of the baggage carousels by the time he arrived. Jimmy scanned the cluster of strangers in search of a face he might recognize from the flight, though it was obvious he was already in the right spot. All the other carousels were empty. Most of the airport, in fact, was empty. It was barely five in the morning and the day was not yet ready to begin. Suddenly he spotted his neighbor on the plane heading in his direction. She was a heavyset woman whose stride was more a waddle than a walk. She had on a crisp, new *sari*. The pale-pink one she wore on the plane had been replaced with a bright blue, perfectly folded and draped around her, revealing only a small section of her robust belly.

She placed her hand thoughtfully on Jimmy's arm when she arrived as if preparing for some profound speech. Jimmy smiled, happy to see her warm, glowing expression again. He waited patiently for her to begin speaking. Perhaps she needed help with something else, he thought. He had helped her figure out the TV on the plane as best he could, walking her through the menus, explaining what her viewing options were before she judiciously decided on a movie fit enough to occupy the many hours from Paris to New Delhi.

Jimmy's smile grew wider as they lingered in silence for a moment longer.

"Thank you, *beta*. All the best on your journey," she said in one swift breath.

"Of course. You're welcome," Jimmy replied. "Thank you," he hollered as she continued her waddle down the long empty hallway toward the exit.

Her sincerity filled Jimmy with a welcome sense of confidence. He had worried about the trip from its inception, fearful he might end up lost or imprisoned in a foreign country, left to survive in a world dauntingly dissimilar from his own. He had read countless travel blogs and watched all the videos he had time to consume on the days leading up to it, taking every precaution to prepare, ready to defend against the many pickpockets and scammers bound to be on the prowl, lurking in corners, waiting to pounce. His passport was buried in a carrying case strapped to his chest, hidden beneath layers of clothing. A wad of safety cash was stashed in his sock, backup money should they get robbed. It all seemed so foolish now that he stood in the perfectly maintained arrivals wing, more modern than most airports in America, patiently waiting for the shimmering metal conveyor belt to begin moving.

"I told you," Luke said as he approached, arms in the air. "Still hasn't started up."

"You were right. Sorry for rushing."

Luke shrugged as he arrived. "You probably should've peed though. I don't know how long it will take to get to the hotel."

"I'm okay. But maybe we should change our cash while we wait," Jimmy suggested, pointing to a nearby booth.

"Okay. I'll just do some for now. I'm sure we can get a better rate outside of the airport."

Jimmy smiled as he watched Luke, wide-awake and skipping toward the booth. He had spent most of the flight asleep on Jimmy's shoulder. Jimmy scarcely slept an hour on the long journey from New York to Paris and Paris to New Delhi. Exhaustion was finally settling in. He was eager to get to the hotel room and crash.

"Done," Luke proclaimed when he returned moments later. The conveyor belt was still motionless. "Wanna slip this in your sock with the rest of the cash?" he whispered in Jimmy's ear, pretending to be suspicious of the imaginary thieves that surrounded them as he safeguarded his pockets. Jimmy jabbed his elbow into Luke's stomach. Luke moaned behind laughter. "You never know. We could get mugged as soon as we step outside."

Jimmy struggled to hold back a smile, rolling his eyes though he knew Luke was right. It was obvious now how much he had overprepared. But Luke had been ever gracious as Jimmy spiraled from one worry to the next, cramming an unnecessary amount of toilet paper and disinfectants into their already bursting backpacks.

A loud, sustained beep blasted through the baggage claim area. A red light flashed above as the conveyor belt hurled into action.

"Finally," Jimmy exclaimed.

"Now let's just hope our bags made it," Luke replied, further egging Jimmy on.

"Don't worry. I've got us covered. If they did get lost in transit, we have everything we need to survive in our backpacks. We're good."

Luke smiled. "I'm sure we are."

GLISTENING GLASS DOORS parted as they exited the airport. A sea of men, held back by metal barriers and ominous police officers, amply armed and stern, flanked the sidewalk holding signs and shouting names mostly foreign to Jimmy's ears. A hint of the chaos Jimmy had read about quickly came into view. His heart began to pound as his eyes scoured through the crowd of drivers.

"How will we know which one is ours?" Luke shouted, his eyes squinting ahead. The clamor grew louder, almost deafening as more passengers hurried to exit, bargaining with drivers and hollering at family members.

"They said he will find us," Jimmy answered, though he began to question the validity of that claim. He had been given no name or description. He had no idea who he was looking for. "Wait here," he told Luke as he moved close to the police officers. He scanned the crowd of men in search of his name on one of the makeshift signs. Suddenly a short, jovial man poked through the mass of people, waving his hand in Jimmy's direction.

"Mr. James," he shouted.

Jimmy smiled brightly at the sight of the man's head emerging through the crowd. He turned to signal Luke who grabbed the bags and scurried toward Jimmy. One of the officers kindly led them across the sidewalk toward the barricade's end.

"This way, this way," the driver continually shouted as he followed along on his side of the barricade. When they finally reached the end of the mosh pit, he approached, taking the bags from Luke. "Mr. James," the kind stranger repeated. "I'm Suresh, your driver."

"Hi, Suresh," Jimmy exclaimed, relieved to be free of the chaos. He extended his hand, shocked at the man's efficiency in seeking him out. Suresh clearly had a leg-up on the group of other men still hollering loudly. "How did you find us so quickly?"

Suresh had little desire to explain his tactics. Instead he smiled and hastily ushered Jimmy and Luke away from the terminal.

"How did he know it was you?" Luke whispered as they made their way across the street toward a large parking lot.

"I have no idea."

They arrived at a tiny red car parked at the far end of the lot and in no time were on their way.

Suresh zoomed through the uninhabited streets of New Delhi with little concern for traffic signs or pedestrians. The early morning fog had created a layer of haze that cast an otherworldly glow across the still landscape. The sun was only just rising, adding a subtle orange tint to the muted shades of brown and gray. Jimmy stared out the window at the wonder that was this new world. His heart raced with excitement at the thought of venturing into the sea of new possibilities. A man approached alongside the tiny red car at one of the few traffic signals Suresh obeyed. He pushed an old wooden cart, its wheels looking like they were on the last leg of its final journey. Jimmy watched as the man shoved the cart to the end of the sidewalk a few feet away. He carefully pulled the dingy tarp off its surface, revealing an array of colorful textiles. The vibrant fabrics sparkled amidst the otherwise dull surroundings, colors beaming brightly, an array of patterns and textures. Jimmy's eyes widened as he poked Luke.

"Amazing," Luke said as he peered through the window. "We're definitely going to do some shopping."

"We really should have brought your dad with us. He could've struck us some deals."

"Now that would've been an adventure. Me, you, and my dad in India."

"This is your first time in India?" Suresh asked, still waiting for the light.

"Yes, it is," Jimmy answered as the light turned green. Suresh revved the engine and the car bolted forward, zooming past the old man and the display of vibrant colors. "And we're very excited to be here."

Jimmy was shocked to find two single beds when they entered the room. A surprisingly strong, young boy hoisted the bags onto luggage racks. "All good?" he asked.

"Actually," Jimmy replied. "I reserved one queen-size bed."

"Yes. We saw two men on the reservation, so we upgraded you to two single beds," the boy replied with a smile. "More comfortable, but don't worry—no extra charge," he said, his head bobbing excitedly.

Luke chuckled at Jimmy slowly winding up, readying for an argument with the hotel employee. "Perfect," Luke interjected, easing his way in front of Jimmy as he tipped the boy. "I'm always up for more comfort."

The boy left smiling, leaving keys on the dresser along with instructions on how to access the Wi-Fi.

Jimmy tossed himself onto one of the beds as he sighed into his palms. "I love that two single beds is an upgrade."

"Hey, it's free of charge," Luke grinned as he approached, hovering over Jimmy. "So, what are we to do about this situation?"

"Push the beds together?" Jimmy suggested.

"Nah, no need," Luke replied as he leaped on top of Jimmy. "We can make this work."

"Yeah, this is perfect." Jimmy kissed Luke's cheeks and chin and nose and lips.

"Do you think we should tell them we're together?" Luke asked. "Maybe they'll upgrade us to the honeymoon suite."

"Or call the cops on us."

Luke laughed as he rolled on to his side. "There's more than enough space for the two of us."

Jimmy turned to his side to face Luke. "I think we'll manage. Besides, it's only for two nights. Then we're off to the next city."

"Let's just hope we don't keep getting upgraded everywhere we go."

Jimmy chuckled, resting his forehead against Luke's.

"You tired?" Luke asked.

Jimmy nodded.

"But it's morning. Don't you have a list of things planned for us?"

"Of course I do. But I need to sleep a little first."

"You wanna mess around? Break in our new beds?"

Jimmy shook his head.

"Okay, let's sleep a little," Luke agreed. "*Then* we can mess around."

"Sounds like a plan," Jimmy said as he turned around and draped Luke's arm across his chest. Luke threw his leg over Jimmy and pulled him closer. "Just maybe an hour or so," Jimmy added with a yawn.

"Sure thing," Luke agreed as he nestled close.

Jimmy locked fingers with Luke, safely at home in the foreign space.

About the Author

Originally from Queens, New York, Daniel Janaka lives in Los Angeles where the excessive sunlight often feels unnatural. Despite living on the West Coast for over a decade, he still gets that warm, tingly feeling whenever he is back in New York. Daniel had his first kiss in Greenwich Village, fell in love in Brooklyn, and walked the lonely streets of Chelsea heartbroken and aimless. The city is where he began his adult life, working in architecture, graphic design, advertising, and eventually post production for television and film. Along the way, Daniel has written numerous short stories and essays recounting his misadventures in growing up and searching for love. MORE PERFECT is his debut novel.

Facebook: www.facebook.com/danieljanaka

Instagram: www.instagram.com/danieljanaka

Website: www.danieljanaka.wordpress.com

Also Available from NineStar Press

Connect with NineStar Press

Website: NineStarPress.com

Facebook: NineStarPress

Facebook Reader Group: NineStarNiche

Twitter: @ninestarpress

Tumblr: NineStarPress

www.ingramcontent.com/pod-product-compliance
Lightning Source LLC
Chambersburg PA
CBHW060544190726
48283CB00003B/866